ERLE STANLEY GARDNER

- Cited by the *Guinness Book of World Records* as the #1 bestselling writer of all time!

- Author of more than 150 clever, authentic, and sophisticated mystery novels!

- Creator of the amazing Perry Mason, the savvy Della Street, and dynamite detective Paul Drake!

- THE ONLY AUTHOR WHO OUTSELLS AGATHA CHRISTIE, HAROLD ROBBINS, BARBARA CARTLAND, AND LOUIS L'AMOUR *COMBINED*!

Why?
Because he writes the best, most fascinating whodunits of all!

You'll want to read every one oɪ them,
from
BALLANTINE BOOKS

By Erle Stanley Gardner
Published by Ballantine Books:

The Case of the
Horrified Heirs

Erle Stanley Gardner

BALLANTINE BOOKS • NEW YORK

146087801

Foreword

A heavy rain in Scotland had swollen the streams. As one of them subsided, a small bundle was left by the receding waters.

This bundle contained human flesh.

A search revealed more bundles. Some of them were found days apart. Apparently, many of them had been thrown from a bridge into the turbulent floodwaters.

Nearly a month after the first discoveries, a left foot was found on the roadside some distance from the stream bed. Nearly a week later, a right forearm with hand was discovered.

All of the recoveries were, of course, in a state of advanced decomposition.

When the pieces were assembled, it was found there were two heads which had been mutilated by removal of eyes, ears, nose, lips and skin. All teeth had been extracted.

It was apparent that a skilled hand had deliberately butchered two human beings in an attempt to make identification humanly impossible.

While visiting in Glasgow, I was privileged to discuss this case with the distinguished medicolegal expert whose work contributed so much to a solution of the murders.

This man is John Glaister, D. Sc., M.D., F.R.S.E. He is learned in the law and in medical science, being a barrister as well as a doctor of science and of medicine. His academic honors, the positions he has held in his long and distinguished career, would make this brief note too long for available space, should I attempt to enumerate them.

Suffice it to say he helped make medicological history by his work in this baffling murder case. The distinguishing features of the bodies were "reconstructed" by scientific methods. Brilliant deduction determined the general neighborhood where the victims had lived, and shrewd detective work resulted in apprehending the murderer.

My friend Professor Glaister is the author of *Medical Jurisprudence and Toxicology* (E. & S. Livingstone, Ltd., Edinburgh & London; 11th Edition), one of the most comprehensive and authoritative books in the field. Those who wish to learn more of the puzzling murder case mentioned, and the scientific methods used to identify the bodies and apprehend the murderer, will find an account of the case in that book.

Professor Glaister is a dedicated man. His is an honored name in his profession. He has contributed much to a science which protects the living by making the dead reveal their secrets. He is a dignified, impartial man, devoid of bias, devoted to finding out the truth, regardless of where the chips may fall.

And so, I dedicate this book to my friend

JOHN GLAISTER, D. Sc., M.D., F.R.S.E.

ERLE STANLEY GARDNER

Chapter 1

Murder is not perpetrated in a vacuum. It is a product of greed, avarice, hate, revenge, or perhaps fear. As a splashing stone sends ripples to the farthest edges of the pond, murder affects the lives of many people.

Early morning sunlight percolated through the window of a private room in the Phillips Memorial Hospital.

Traffic noises in the street, which had been hushed to a low hum during the night, began to swell in volume. The steps of nurses in the corridors increased in tempo, indicating an increase in the workload.

Patients were being washed, temperatures taken, blood samples collected; then the breakfast trays came rolling along, the faint aroma of coffee and oatmeal seeped into the corridors, as if apologetically asking permission to push aside the aura of antiseptic severity, promising that the intrusion would be only temporary.

Nurses holding sterile hypodermic syringes hurried into the rooms of surgery patients, giving the preliminary quieting drug which would allay apprehensions and pave the way for the anesthetic.

Lauretta Trent sat up in bed and smiled wanly at the nurse.

"I feel better," she proclaimed in a weak voice.

"Doctor promised to look in this morning right after surgery," the nurse told her, smiling reassuringly.

"He said I could go home?" the patient asked eagerly.

"You'll have to ask him about that," the nurse said. "But

1

you're going to have to watch your diet for a while. This last upset was very, very bad indeed."

Lauretta sighed. "I wish I knew what was causing them. I've tried to be careful. I must be developing some sort of an allergy."

Chapter 2

Out at the Trent residence, set in its spacious grounds reminiscent of a bygone era, the housekeeper was putting the finishing touches on the master bedroom.

"They say Mrs. Trent will be home today," she said to the maid. "The doctor asked her nurse, Anna Fritch, to be here, and she has just arrived. She'll stay for a week or two this time."

The maid was unenthusiastic. "Just my luck. I wanted to get off this afternoon—it's something special."

It was at this moment that a pair of hands hovered briefly over the washbowl in a tiled bathroom.

A trickle of white powder descended from a phial into the bowl.

One of the hands turned on a water faucet and the white powder drained down the wastepipe.

There would be no more need for this powder. It had served its purpose.

Over the spacious house was an air of tense expectancy as various people waited: Boring Briggs, Lauretta's brother-in-law; Dianne, his wife; Gordon Kelvin; another brother-in-law; and Maxine, his wife; the housekeeper, the maid, the cook; the nurse; George Eagan, the chauffeur. Each affected differently by the impending return of Lauretta Trent, they collectively managed to permeate the atmosphere with suppressed excitement.

Now that the morning surgery was over and the surgeons had changed to street clothes, there was a lull in the activities at the Phillips Memorial Hospital.

The patients who had been through surgery were in the recovery room; the first of them, recovering from the more minor operations, were beginning to trickle through the corridors, eyes closed, faces pale, covered with blankets as they were wheeled to their respective rooms.

Dr. Ferris Alton, medium height, slim-waisted despite his fifty-eight years, walked down to the private room of Lauretta Trent.

Her face lit up as the doctor opened the swinging door.

The nurse looked over her shoulder, and seeing Dr. Alton, moved swiftly to the foot of the bed, where she stood waiting at attention.

Dr. Alton smiled at his patient. "You're better this morning."

"Much, much better," she said. "Am I to go home today?"

"You're going home," Dr. Alton said, "but you're going to have your old nurse, Anna Fritch, back with you. I've arranged for her to have the adjoining bedroom. Technically, she'll be on duty twenty-four hours a day. I want her to keep an eye on you. We shouldn't have let her go after that last upset. I want her to keep an eye on your heart."

Mrs. Trent nodded.

"Now then," Dr. Alton went on, "I'm going to be frank with you, Lauretta. This is the third gastroenteric upset in eight months. They're bad enough in themselves, but it's your heart that I'm concerned about. It won't stand these dietary indiscretions indefinitely. You're going to *have* to watch your diet."

"I know," she told him, "but there are times when the spiced food tastes so *darn* good."

He frowned at her, regarding her thoughtfully.

"I think," he said at length, "when you're more yourself we'll have a series of allergy tests. In the meantime, you're going to have to be careful. I think it's only fair to warn you that your heart may not be able to stand another of these acute disturbances."

Chapter 3

The hands and the powder had done their work. The way had been paved; the preliminaries were all out of the way.

Lauretta Trent's life depended upon a woman she had seen only once, a woman whose very existence she had forgotten about; and this woman, Virginia Baxter, had only a vague recollection of Lauretta Trent. She had met the older woman briefly ten years ago as a matter of routine.

If she tried, Virginia could probably have recalled the meeting but it was now entirely submerged in her mind, buried under the day-to-day experiences of a decade of routine problems.

Now Virginia was following the stream of passengers filing past the airline stewardesses.

"Goodbye."

"Bye now."

"Goodbye, sir."

"Goodbye. Nice trip."

"Thank you. Goodbye."

The passengers left the jet plane, inched their way to the broader corridors of the airport, then quickened their pace, walking down the long runway toward a huge illuminated sign bearing the word "Baggage," with an arrow pointing downward where an escalator descended to a lower level.

Virginia Baxter steadied herself by putting her right hand on the rail of the escalator.

She was carrying a topcoat over her arm, and she was tired.

In her late thirties, she had retained a trim figure and a

way with clothes, but she had worked hard during her life and minute crow's feet were beginning to appear at the corners of her eyes; there was just a suggestion of a faint line on each side of her nose. When she smiled, her face lit up; when it was in repose, there were times when the corners of her mouth began to sag ever so slightly.

She stepped from the escalator at the lower level and walked briskly toward the revolving platform on which the baggage would appear.

It was too early, as yet, for the baggage to make its appearance, but it was indicative of Virginia's character that she walked with nervously rapid steps, hurrying to reach the place where she would wait for several long minutes.

At length, baggage began to appear on a moving belt; the belt transported the baggage to the slowly revolving turntable.

Passengers began to pick out baggage; porters with claim checks stood by, occasionally pulling out heavy handbags and putting them on hand trucks.

The crowd began to thin out. Finally, only a few pieces of baggage were left on the turntable. The trucks had moved away. Virginia's baggage was not in sight.

She moved over to a porter. "My baggage didn't come in," she said.

"What was it, lady?" he asked.

"A single suitcase, brown, and a small oblong overnight case for cosmetics."

"Let me see your checks, please."

She handed him the baggage checks.

He said, "Before I start looking, we'd better wait and see if there's another truck coming. Sometimes there's a second section of trucks when there's an unusually large load."

Virginia waited impatiently.

After two or three minutes, more baggage showed up on the moving belt. There were four suitcases, Virginia's and two others.

"There they are now! Those two are mine," she said. "The brown one—the big one in front—and the oblong overnight bag in back."

"Okay, ma'am. I'll get them for you."

The suitcase, followed by the overnight bag, moved along the conveyor belt, then hit the slide to the revolving table. A few seconds later, the porter picked them up, compared the tags for a moment, put the bags on his hand truck and started for the door.

A man who had been standing well back came forward. "Just a moment, please," he said.

The porter looked at him. The man produced a leather folder from his side pocket and opened it, showing a gold shield. "Police," he said. "Was there some trouble about this baggage?"

"No trouble," the porter hastily assured him. "No trouble at all, sir. It just didn't come in with the first load."

"There's been some baggage trouble," the man said to Virginia Baxter. "This is your suitcase?"

"Yes."

"You're sure of it?"

"Of course. That's my suitcase and overnight bag and I gave the checks for them to the porter."

"Could you describe the contents of the suitcase?"

"Why, certainly."

"Will you please do so?"

"Well, on top there's a three-quarter-length beige coat with a brown fur collar; there's a checked skirt and—"

"That will give us enough of a description to make sure," the man said. "Would you mind opening it up just so I can look inside?"

Virginia hesitated for a moment, then said, "Well, I guess it's all right."

"Is it locked?"

"No, I just have it closed."

The man snapped back the catches.

7

The porter lowered the truck so the suitcase would be level.

Virginia raised the cover and then recoiled at what she saw on the inside.

Her three-quarter-length coat was there, neatly folded, just as she had left it, but on top of the coat were several transparent plastic containers and inside these containers, neatly wrapped, an assortment of small packages.

"You didn't tell me about these," the man said. "What are they?"

"I . . . I don't know. I never saw them before in my life."

As though at a signal, a man with a press camera and a flash gun materialized from behind one of the pillars.

While Virginia was still trying to compose herself, the camera was thrust up into her face and her eyes were blinded by a brilliant flash of light.

The man, working with swift efficiency, ejected the bulb from the flash gun, inserted another bulb, pulled a slide back and forth on the back of the camera, and took another picture of the open suitcase.

The porter had backed hastily away so that he was not included in the pictures.

The officer said, "I'm afraid, madam, you're going to have to come with me."

"What do you mean?"

"I'll explain it," the officer said. "Your name is Virginia Baxter?"

"Yes. Why?"

"We've had a tip on you," the officer said. "We were told that you traffick in narcotics."

The photographer took one more picture, then turned and scurried away.

Virginia said to the officer, "Why, of course I'll come with you, if you're going to try to clear this up. I haven't the faintest idea of how that stuff got in my suitcase."

"I see," the officer said, gravely. "You'll have to come to

headquarters, I'm afraid. We'll have that stuff analyzed and see exactly what it is."

"And if it should turn out to be—narcotics?"

"Then we'll have to book you."

"But that's—that's crazy!"

"Bring the bags this way," the officer said to the porter, closing the suitcase.

He opened the overnight bag, disclosing jars of cream, a manicure set, a negligee, some bottles of lotion.

"Okay," he said. "This is all right, I guess, but we'll have to look in these jars and bottles. We'll just take both bags along with us."

He escorted Virginia to a plain black sedan, had the porter hoist the suitcase and overnight bag into the rear seat, put Virginia in the seat behind him and started the motor.

"You're going to headquarters?"

"Yes."

Virginia noticed then that there was a police radio in the car. The officer picked up the microphone and said, "Special Officer Jack Andrews leaving the airport with a female suspect and a suitcase containing suspicious material to be checked. Time is 10:17 A.M."

The officer replaced the microphone on a hook, pulled away from the curb, and guided the car expertly and swiftly in the direction of headquarters.

There Virginia was placed in charge of a policewoman and kept waiting for around fifteen minutes, then an officer delivered a folded paper to the policewoman. She looked at it and said, "This way, please."

Virginia followed her to a desk. "Your right hand, please."

The policewoman took Virginia's right hand before she realized what was happening, then grasping the thumb firmly, rolled it over a big pad and placed it on a piece of paper, rolling out a fingerprint.

"Now, the next finger," she said.

9

"You can't fingerprint me," Virginia said, pulling back. "Why, I—"

The grip on the finger tightened. "Now, just don't make it hard on yourself," the policewoman said. "The index finger, please."

"I refuse!— Good heavens, what have I done?" Virginia asked. "I— Why, this is a nightmare."

"You're privileged to make a telephone call," the woman said. "You can call an attorney, if you wish."

The words clicked in Virginia's mind.

"Where is a telephone directory?" she asked. "I want the office of Perry Mason."

A few moments later, Virginia had Della Street, Perry Mason's confidential secretary, on the line.

"May I speak with Perry Mason, please?"

"You'll have to tell me what it's about," Della Street said, "perhaps I can help you."

"I'm Virginia Baxter," she said. "I worked for Delano Bannock, the attorney, during his lifetime and up to his death a couple of years ago. I've seen Mr. Mason two or three times. He came to Mr. Bannock's office. He may remember me; I was the secretary and receptionist."

"I see," Della said. "What is the present problem, Miss Baxter?"

"I'm arrested for having narcotics in my possession," she said, "and I haven't the faintest idea of how they got there. I need Mr. Mason at once."

"Just a minute," Della said.

A moment later, Perry Mason's deep but well-modulated voice was on the line. "Where are you, Miss Baxter?"

"I'm at headquarters."

"Tell them to hold you right there, if they will, please," Mason said. "I'm on my way."

"Oh, thank you. Thank you so much. I . . . I just haven't any idea how this happened and—"

"Never mind trying to explain over the telephone," Mason told her. "Don't say anything to anyone except to tell them to hold you right there, that I'm on my way. How are you fixed for bail? Could you put up bail?"

"I ... if it isn't too high. I have a little property, not much."

"I'm on my way up," Mason said. "I want to demand that you be taken before the nearest and most accessible magistrate immediately. Just sit tight."

Chapter 4

Perry Mason invaded Virginia Baxter's nightmare and tore aside the web of unreality and terror.

"The magistrate has fixed bail at five thousand dollars," Mason said. "Can you raise that?"

"I'd have to draw out all of my checking account and withdraw money from the building and loan."

"That would be better than waiting in jail," Mason pointed out. "Now then, I want to know exactly what happened."

Virginia told him the events of the morning.

"You were on the plane, coming from where?"

"From San Francisco."

"What had you been doing in San Francisco?"

"I was visiting my aunt. I've been to see her several times lately. She's elderly, not at all well and she's all alone. She likes my visits."

"What are you doing? Are you working for a living?"

"Not steadily. I haven't been regularly employed since Mr. Bannock died. I have taken a few odd jobs."

"I take it, then, you have some income?" Mason asked.

"Yes," she said. "Mr. Bannock had no relatives, other than the one brother. He remembered me in his will. He gave me a piece of real property in Hollywood that produces an income and—"

"How long had you been with Bannock?"

"Fifteen years," she said. "I started working for him when I was twenty."

"You've been married?"

"Yes, once. It didn't take."

"Divorced?"

"No. We're separated, have been for some time."

"Friendly with your husband?"

"No."

"What's his name?"

"Colton Baxter."

"You go by the title 'Miss'?"

"Yes. I think it helps in secretarial employment."

"Now, you'd been to see your aunt. You got aboard that plane. What about the baggage? Anything unusual about the checking of the baggage?"

"No— Wait a minute, I had to pay excess baggage."

Mason's eyes showed swift interest. "You paid excess baggage?"

"Yes."

"Do you have your receipt?"

"It's attached to my ticket. That's in my purse. They took my purse away from me when I was booked."

"We'll get it back," Mason said. "Now then, you were traveling alone?"

"Yes."

"Remember anything about the person you were seated next to?"

"He was a man of about thirty-two or thirty-three, rather well-dressed but— Well, now that I stop to think of it, he was ... well, there was something peculiar about him. He was cold, rather crisp in his manner, not like the ordinary passenger you encounter on those trips. It's hard to explain what I mean."

"Would you know him if you saw him again?" Mason asked.

"Yes, indeed."

"Could you identify him from a photograph?"

"I think so, if it's a clear photograph."

"You only had the one suitcase?" Mason asked.

"No, I had a suitcase and an overnight bag, an oblong bag containing cosmetics."

"What became of that?"

"They took it. The suitcase came through first. The porter picked it up and then picked up the overnight bag. At that moment, a man stepped forward and showed me his identification card and asked me if I had any objections to his taking a quick look in my suitcase because there had been some trouble. Since my baggage had been delayed coming off the plane, I thought that was what he referred to."

"What did you tell him?"

"I told him what was in the suitcase and that it was all right for him to look."

"Can you remember anything more about the conversation?"

"Yes. He asked me first if that was my suitcase, and I told him it was, and he asked me if I could establish my ownership by identifying the contents. Then I described the contents, and he asked if it was all right to check."

Mason frowned thoughtfully, then said, almost casually, "Your baggage, that is, the two pieces together, weighed more than forty pounds?"

"Yes. They weighed forty-six pounds taken together, and I paid excess baggage on the six pounds."

"I see," Mason said thoughtfully. "You're going to have to exercise a lot of self-control, and you're in for a disagreeable experience, but perhaps we can work things out one way or another."

"What I can't understand," she said, "is where the stuff came from and how it could have been placed in my suitcase. Of course, it was late coming off the plane, but one wouldn't think anyone could tamper with it out there on the field going from the plane to the baggage counter."

"There were several places it *could* have been tampered

14

with," Mason said. "After you checked the suitcase and before it was put on the plane, someone could have opened it.

"We don't know where it was stored aboard the plane in the baggage compartment. We don't *know* whether anyone could have tampered with it in there.

"Then, of course, when it was taken off the plane, there was this delay. That means that the suitcase was probably placed on the ground, waiting for another truck to come along to pick it up. Now, the way those planes are built, the baggage comes out on the other side from the side which has the passenger entrance. While the suitcase was there on the ground, it wouldn't have been too difficult for someone to have opened it and inserted these packages of narcotics."

"But why?" she asked.

"There," Mason said, "is the rub. Presumably someone was trafficking in narcotics. He knew there'd been a tip-off and his baggage was going to be searched, so he put the contraband in your suitcase and then had an accomplice telephone the police that the stuff would be in the suitcase of one Virginia Baxter. He must have been able to describe you, because the officer who was standing there waiting for you to claim your baggage evidently had a good description of you and had you spotted from the time he saw you come down the escalator."

Mason was thoughtful for a moment, then said, "How about your name? How did you have your suitcase marked? Was there an initial or a name painted on it, or what?"

"There's a leather baggage tag," she said, "one that straps around the ring at the handle, and it had my name typed on it, my name and address: 422 Eureka Arms Apartments."

"All right," Mason said, "we'll get you out on bail. I'm going to try and have you brought up on a preliminary hearing just as soon as possible. At least we'll make the police show their hand.

"I'm satisfied it's all some sort of a mistake and we *may*

be able to get it cleaned up without much trouble, but you're going to have to put up with a lot of things."

"Tell me," she asked apprehensively, "there was a photographer there. Will there be anything in the newspapers about it?"

"A photographer?" Mason asked.

She nodded.

Mason said grimly, "Then the thing is a lot more sinister than I had at first supposed. It isn't just a simple mistake. Yes, it will be in the newspapers."

"My name, address, everything?"

"Name, address and photograph," Mason said. "Prepare yourself for a picture showing the startled expression on your face and a caption such as: Ex-legal secretary accused in narcotics charge."

"But how could the newspapers have had a photographer there?"

"That's just the point," Mason said. "Some officers like publicity. In return for publicity, they give some friendly newspaper reporter a tip when they're going to make an arrest of some young woman who is photogenic.

"The newspapers play up the story, the officer gets his name in the paper with a favorable bit of publicity. Under these circumstances, be prepared to read that the value of the narcotics in your suitcase, at current retail prices, amounted to several thousand dollars."

Her face showed her dismay.

"And after I'm acquitted," she asked, "then what will happen?"

"Probably nothing," Mason said. "Perhaps a few lines on an inside page of a newspaper."

"I *will* be acquitted, won't I?" she asked hopefully.

Mason said, "I'm an attorney, not a fortuneteller. We'll do our best and you'll have to let it go at that."

Chapter 5

Mason escorted Virginia Baxter to a seat inside the rail of the courtroom.

"Now, don't be nervous," he said reassuringly.

She said, "That's like telling a cold person not to shiver. I can't help being nervous. I'm shaking like a leaf on the inside, if not on the outside. I feel full of butterflies."

Mason said, "This is a preliminary hearing. It is usually a matter of routine for the judge to bind a defendant over to the higher court. When he does that, he quite frequently increases the amount of bail. Sometimes he makes the bail almost prohibitive. You're going to have to face that possibility."

"I just can't raise any more bail, Mr. Mason, that's all, unless I sell my real property at a loss."

"I know," Mason said. "I'm just telling you what *may* happen. However, real property in your name will influence a judge in fixing the amount of bail."

"You don't hold out much hope of . . . getting me out on this preliminary hearing?"

"Ordinarily," Mason said, "the judge binds the defendant over if the prosecutor wants to go ahead with the case in the higher court. Sometimes, of course, we get a break.

"It's almost unheard of to put a defendant on the stand at the time of a preliminary examination, but if I think there's even a faint chance of getting the judge to dismiss the case, I'm going to put you on the stand so he can take a look at you and see the kind of person you really are."

"That horrid newspaper story," she said, "—and that picture!"

"From the city editor's standpoint, it was a wonderful picture," Mason said. "It showed surprise and consternation on your face and, as far as your case is concerned, the picture may do you some good."

"But it blasted my reputation," she said. "My friends are avoiding me in a big way."

Mason started to say something but checked himself as the door of the judge's chambers opened.

"Stand up," Mason said.

Every person in the courtroom arose as Judge Cortland Albert took his seat at the bench, then glanced appraisingly at the defendant.

"This is the time heretofore fixed for the preliminary hearing in the case of the People versus Virginia Baxter. Are you ready to proceed?"

"Ready for the defendant," Mason said.

Jerry Caswell, one of the younger trial deputies who was frequently sent in to handle preliminary hearings and who was eagerly trying to make a record which would attract the attention of his superiors, was on his feet.

"The prosecution," he announced dramatically, "is *always* ready!"

He waited a moment, then seated himself.

"Call your first witness," Judge Albert said.

Caswell called the porter from the airport.

"Are you acquainted with the defendant?"

"Yes, sir. I saw her."

"On the seventeenth of this month?"

"Yes, sir."

"You are one of the porters at the airport?"

"Yes, sir."

"And you make a living from transporting baggage?"

"Yes, sir."

18

"Now, did the defendant, on the seventeenth of this month, indicate to you a suitcase?"

"She did. Yes, sir."

"Would you know that suitcase if you saw it again?"

"I would. Yes, sir."

Caswell nodded to a police officer who came forward with the suitcase.

"Is that the one?"

"Yes, sir, that's the one."

"I want that marked 'People's Exhibit A' for identification," Caswell said.

"So ordered," the judge ruled.

"And the defendant said that was her suitcase?"

"Yes, sir."

"Were you present when the suitcase was opened?"

"Yes, sir."

"What was in the suitcase when it was opened, other than clothes, if anything?"

"There were some packages done up in plastic."

"How many? Do you know?"

"I didn't count them. There was a goodly number."

"That's all," Caswell said. "Cross-examine."

"The defendant identified this suitcase as being hers?" Mason asked.

"Yes, sir."

"Did she give you a baggage check?"

"She did. Yes, sir."

"And you compared the number on the check given you by the defendant with the number on the suitcase?"

"Yes, sir."

"How many checks did the defendant give you?"

"Actually, she gave me two."

"What became of the second check?"

"That was for an overnight bag. I got that for her, too."

"And was that opened?"

"Yes, sir."

"Now, directing your attention to the suitcase, just prior to the time the suitcase was opened, was there some conversation with a person who identified himself as a police officer?"

"Yes, sir. Officer Jack Andrews showed this young woman his credentials and asked her if that was her suitcase."

"What did she say?"

"She said it was."

"And what did Andrews say?"

"He asked her if he could open it."

"No other conversation?"

"Well, that was the substance of it."

"I'm not asking you about the substance," Mason said. "I'm asking you about the conversation itself. Didn't he ask her if she was positive that was her suitcase, and if she could identify the suitcase by describing the articles that were in it?"

"Yes, sir, that's right."

"And then he asked her to open the suitcase so he could inspect those articles?"

"Yes, sir."

"And what about the overnight bag? Did he ask her to identify that?"

"He just asked her if it was hers."

"And she said it was?"

"Yes."

"And then what happened?"

"He opened it."

"That's all?"

"Well, of course, afterwards they took her away with them."

"Now, I call your attention to a photograph in an evening edition of the newspaper published on the seventeenth, and call your attention to this picture of the defendant and the suitcase."

"Objected to as incompetent, irrelevant and immaterial and not proper cross-examination," Caswell said.

"It is preliminary only and for the purpose of bringing out part of the *res gestae*," Mason said.

"Overruled. I'll hear it," Judge Albert announced.

"Were you present when this picture was taken?"

"Yes, sir."

"Did you see the photographer?"

"Yes, sir."

"Where did he come from?"

"He was hiding behind one of the pillars."

"And when the suitcase was opened, he came out with his camera?"

"Yes, sir. He darted out from behind that pillar with his camera all ready, and *boom—boom—boom* he took three pictures."

"And then what?"

"Then he ran away."

"If the Court please," Caswell said, "we move to strike out all this testimony about the photographer. Not only is it improper cross-examination but it is incompetent, irrelevant and immaterial. It serves no useful purpose."

"It serves a very useful purpose, if the Court please," Mason rejoined. "It shows that this was no mere casual search. It shows that the officer had planned the search and anticipated what he was going to find. He had tipped off a friendly newspaper reporter and, if the Court will read the article in this newspaper, it will be seen that the reporter endeavored to reciprocate by seeing that the officer had proper publicity in return for the favor extended."

Judge Albert smiled very slightly.

"Your Honor, I object. I object to any such statement," Caswell said.

"It is merely by way of argument," Mason said.

"An argument for what purpose?" Caswell asked.

"To show the relevancy of the testimony," Mason said.

"To show that the officer was acting under some specific tip, some bit of information which had been given to him; and the defense proposes to find out what that information was and who gave it to him."

A look of fleeting dismay appeared on Caswell's features.

Judge Albert smiled and said, "I thought I appreciated the underlying purpose of the cross-examination when counsel started asking the questions. The motion to strike is denied.

"Do you have any further cross-examination, Mr. Mason?"

"No, Your Honor."

"Redirect?"

"No, Your Honor," Jerry Caswell said.

"Call your next witness."

Caswell said, "I call Detective Jack Andrews.

"What is your name?" Caswell asked after Andrews had been sworn.

"Jackman, J-A-C-K-M-A-N, Andrews. I am known generally as Jack Andrews, but Jackman is my name."

"Directing your attention to the suitcase which has been marked for identification as People's Exhibit A, when did you first see that suitcase?"

"When the defendant pointed it out to the porter who has just testified."

"And what did you do?"

"I approached her and asked her if that was her suitcase."

"And then what?"

"I asked her if she had any objection to my looking in the suitcase and she said she did not."

"And then what happened?"

"I opened the suitcase."

"And what did you find?"

"I found fifty packages of—"

"Now, just a moment," Mason interrupted. "I submit, if the Court please, this particular question has now been asked and fully answered. The witness said he found fifty packages. As to the contents of these packages, that is another matter and calls for another question."

"Very well," Caswell said. "If counsel wants to do it the hard way, we'll do it the hard way. Now, did you take those packages into your possession?"

"I did."

"And did you take steps to ascertain what those packages were, what the substance consisted of?"

"I did."

"And what was the substance?"

"Now, just a moment," Mason said. "At this point, we interpose an objection on the ground that it is incompetent, irrelevant and immaterial; that no proper foundation has been laid; that the property was taken as the result of an illegal search and seizure, and is incompetent as evidence in this case.

"In this connection, if the Court please, I desire to ask a few questions."

"Very well, in connection with this objection which has been made, you may take the witness on *voir dire*."

"Did you have a search warrant?" Mason asked the witness.

"No, sir, there wasn't time to get a search warrant."

"You just went out there?"

"I just went out there, but I call your attention to the fact that I asked the defendant *if she had any objection to* my looking in the suitcase and she said it was all right, to go right ahead."

"Now, just a minute," Mason said. "You're relating the substance of the conversation. You're giving your conclusion as to what the conversation consisted of. Can you remember your exact words?"

"Well, those were virtually my exact words."

"Did you tell her you wanted to search her suitcase?"

"Yes."

"Now, just a minute," Mason said. "You're under oath. Did you tell her you wanted to search her suitcase, or did you ask her if she could identify the contents of the suitcase?"

"I believe I asked her if it was her suitcase and she said it was, and I asked her if she could describe the contents and she described them."

"And then you asked her if she had any objection to opening the suitcase *in order to show you the contents she had described.* Isn't that right?"

"Yes, sir."

"But you didn't tell her you wanted to *search* the suitcase?"

"No."

"She gave you no permission to search the suitcase?"

"She said it would be all right to open it."

"She gave you no permission to search the suitcase?"

"I told her I wanted to open it and she said it would be all right."

"She gave you no permission to search the suitcase?"

"Well, I guess the word 'search' wasn't mentioned."

"Exactly," Mason said. "Now, you went down to wait for this defendant at the airline terminal in response to a tip, did you not?"

"Well . . . yes."

"Who gave you that tip?"

"I'm not in a position to disclose the sources of our information."

"I think under the present rulings of the courts," Mason said, "this witness must show that he had reasonable grounds for wanting to search that suitcase, and an anonymous tip, or one from a person he didn't know, wouldn't constitute reasonable grounds of search; therefore, the defendant is entitled to know the reasons for which he wanted to search the suitcase."

Judge Albert frowned, turned to the witness. "Do you refuse to disclose the name of the person giving you the tip?"

"The tip didn't come to me," Andrews said. "It came to one of my superiors. I was told that there had been a hot tip and to go down to the airport, to wait for this party and see if I could get permission to look in the suitcase. If I couldn't, I was to keep her under surveillance until a warrant could be obtained."

Judge Albert said, "This is an interesting situation. Apparently, the defendant did not give anyone permission to 'search' the suitcase but did give her consent to opening the suitcase for the sole purpose of demonstrating the presence of certain articles. It's a peculiar situation."

"I'll get at it in still another way, if the Court please," Mason said. "I want to make the defendant's position plain. We would like to get this matter cleaned up in this preliminary hearing and not on some technicality."

Mason turned to the witness. "You took fifty packages out of that suitcase?"

"Yes, sir."

"You have them here in court?"

"Yes, sir."

"Did you weigh them?"

"Weigh them? No, sir. We counted the packages and made our inventory that way rather than by weight."

"Now, there was a second bag, an overnight bag?"

"Yes, sir."

"Did you ask the defendant to identify that?"

"She said it was hers. She had a claim check for it."

"And did you ask her about the contents?"

"No."

"Did you ask her if it would be all right to open it?"

"No."

"But you did open it and search it?"

"Yes. However, we found nothing significant in that overnight bag."

"You didn't ask her permission to open that bag?"

"I don't believe I did."

"You just went ahead and opened it anyway?"

"That was after I'd found this big shipment of—"

Mason held up his hand. "Never mind what it was, at this time," he said. "We'll refer to it simply as 'fifty packages.' What did you do with the overnight bag?"

"We have it here."

"Now then," Mason said, "since you don't know how much the fifty packages weighed, do you know how much the suitcase weighed without the fifty packages?"

"I do not."

"Did you know the defendant had paid excess baggage on the suitcases?"

"Yes."

"Yet you never weighed them?"

"No."

"I suggest, if the Court please, we weigh them now," Mason said.

"What is the purpose of this offer?" Judge Albert inquired.

"If," Mason said, "the scales show that these two bags, at the present time, and *without* the packages, weigh forty-six pounds, then it is conclusive evidence that someone planted whatever was in that suitcase *after it had left the possession of the defendant.*"

"I think the point is well taken," Judge Albert said. "I'm going to take a recess for ten minutes. The bailiff will have some scales brought into court and we will weigh those two suitcases."

"That doesn't necessarily mean anything," Caswell protested. "We only have the defendant's word that they weighed forty-six pounds. She has been out on bail. We don't know what has been taken from those suitcases."

"Haven't they been in the custody of the police?" Judge Albert asked.

"Yes, but there would have been no objection to her going to the suitcase to take clothes."

"*Did* she go to the suitcase and take anything?"

"I don't know, Your Honor."

"If you don't know whether she took something out, you don't know whether someone else put something in," Judge Albert snapped. "The Court will take a recess of ten minutes and we'll have scales brought in."

Mason sauntered out to a telephone booth, called the pressroom at headquarters and said, "An interesting demonstration is taking place in court in ten minutes. Judge Cortland Albert is going to weigh the evidence."

"Doesn't he always weigh the evidence?" one of the reporters asked facetiously.

"Not this way," Mason said. "He's going to weigh it with a pair of scales."

"What?"

"That's right. With a pair of scales, in ten minutes. You'd better be up here. You might get something good."

"What department?" the reporter asked.

Mason told him.

"We'll be up," the man said. "Hold it off a little if you can."

"I can't," Mason told him. "As soon as the judge gets the scales in, he's going to reconvene court. He thinks he can do it within ten minutes and I think he can, too. The bailiff is getting the scales."

Mason hung up.

Chapter 6

Mason, standing beside Virginia Baxter, said, "I'm gambling everything on the fact that you're telling the truth. If you're lying, you're going to get hurt."

"I'm not lying, Mr. Mason."

Mason said, "Ordinarily, at the time of arrest, there would be a dramatic picture on the front page showing an ex–legal secretary smuggling dope. Dismissal of the charges at a preliminary hearing would rate about five or six lines buried somewhere in the inner pages of the paper.

"What I'm trying to do is to make this thing so dramatic that it will be a big story in itself. If you're telling the truth, we'll vindicate your name in such a way that everyone who read the original article and remembered it will read this one and remember that you were acquitted of the charge.

"But if you're lying, this test is going to crucify you."

"Mr. Mason, I'm telling you the absolute truth. Why in the world would I want to peddle dope, or get mixed up in it in any way?"

Mason grinned and said, "I don't ask myself all those questions usually; I just say, 'This girl is my client and, as such, she has to be right. At least, I'm going to act on that assumption.' "

The bailiff and two deputies appeared trundling a platform scale, taken from the jail building and used to weigh prisoners at the time they were booked.

The bailiff vanished into Judge Albert's chambers to report.

The swinging doors of the courtroom were pushed open

as half a dozen reporters accompanied by photographers entered the courtroom.

One of the reporters approached Mason. "Would you and your client pose by the scales?" he asked.

"I won't," Mason said. "My client will, but I think you will have to wait until court is adjourned—and by that time, there's just a chance Judge Albert might pose with you."

"Why won't you pose?" the reporter asked.

"It's not supposed to be ethical," Mason said.

The reporter's face flushed with anger. "That's the bar association for you," he said. "Appointing committees, trying to get better public relations, and then trying to hide behind a false front of legal ethics.

"When will you lawyers learn that public relations simply means taking the public into partnership and letting newspaper readers look over your shoulders and see what you're doing?

"Any time the lawyers are too stuffy or too afraid to let the public know what they're doing, they're going to have poor public relations."

Mason grinned and said, "Calm down, buddy. I'm not stopping you from looking over my shoulder, I'm simply stopping you from looking at my face with a camera and flashlight. That's supposed to be unethical advertising—not that I give a damn, but I'm leaning over backwards. However, as far as the story is concerned, why the hell do you suppose I went to all the trouble of setting this up?"

The angry reporter looked at him, then his face softened in a grin. "I guess you're right at that," he said. "Is the judge actually going to weigh the evidence?"

"Going to weigh the physical evidence," Mason said.

"Cripes, what a story!" the reporter commented, just as the door from chambers opened and the bailiff said, "Everybody stand up."

The audience arose, and Judge Albert entered the courtroom, noticing, with a touch of amusement and some surprise, the manner in which the courtroom, which had been almost empty, had now filled up nearly to capacity with spectators from the various county offices, newspaper reporters and photographers.

"People versus Virginia Baxter," he said. "Are we ready to proceed?"

"Ready, Your Honor," Caswell said.

"Ready for the defendant," Mason announced.

Detective Jack Andrews was on the stand and the evidence was about to be weighed. "You have scales, Mr. Bailiff?"

"Yes, Your Honor."

"Check them, please, and see if they are accurate. Put them on zero and watch the beam."

The bailiff checked the scales.

"All right," Judge Albert directed, "now, let's have the suitcase and the overnight bag put on the scales."

The clerk took the two bags which had been marked for identification, placed them on the scales and carefully adjusted the beam until it balanced, then stood back.

"Exactly forty-six and one-quarter pounds, Your Honor," the bailiff announced.

There was a moment of tense, dramatic silence and then someone applauded.

Judge Albert frowned and said, "We'll have no demonstrations, please. Now, does the defendant have the airplane ticket and the receipt for the excess baggage?"

"We have, Your Honor," Mason said, handing the ticket and the receipt to Judge Albert.

Judge Albert frowned at the assistant prosecutor. "How much does the material weigh that was taken out of the bags?"

"I don't know, Your Honor. As the witness Andrews testified, it was counted by packages and not weighed."

30

"All right, let's weigh it," Judge Albert said. "You have it here in court?"

"Yes, Your Honor."

The bailiff started to remove the baggage from the scales.

Mason said, "If the Court please, I would prefer to have these articles simply placed on top of the bags while they are on the scales and we will then see how much it increases the weight."

"Very well," Judge Albert ruled. "It's just as easy one way as the other, perhaps a little more dramatic and, therefore, a little more convincing to have it done as counsel suggests."

Officer Andrews produced a bag with the cellophane-wrapped packages and, taking the packages from the bag, placed them on top of the suitcases.

The arm of the scale quivered, then went upwards.

The bailiff adjusted the sliding weight.

"One pound and three-quarters, Your Honor," he announced.

Judge Albert glanced at the prosecutor, then at Andrews. "Does the prosecution have any explanation for this?" he asked.

"No, Your Honor," Jerry Caswell said. "We feel that the material was found in the defendant's suitcase and therefore that she's responsible for it. After all, there was nothing to prevent her adding this material after the baggage had been weighed. She could have done it as easily as anyone else could have done it."

"Not so easy," Judge Albert said. "When suitcases are checked on an airline, they're weighed on the scale at the time the passenger checks in, and the ticket clerk then takes them from the scale and sends them out to the airline.

"As far as this Court is concerned, the evidence is convincing and the case is dismissed."

Judge Albert stood up, looked down at the courtroom

where people were still coming in through the doors and said, with a slight smile, "Court is adjourned."

One of the reporters rushed forward. "Your Honor, would you consider posing in front of the scale? We want to get a story and a picture, and we'd like to have some human interest."

Judge Albert hesitated.

"No objection whatever on the part of the defendant," Mason announced in a loud voice.

Judge Albert looked at Jerry Caswell.

Caswell avoided his glance.

Judge Albert smiled. "Well, if you want to have human interest, you'd better have the defendant standing beside me and pointing out that it's her baggage that's being weighed."

The reporters and photographers gathered around the scales.

"And let it appear that these pictures were taken after court had adjourned," Judge Albert said. "I've always been broadminded about publicity photographs in my court, although I know there are judges who object. However, I am not entirely unaware of the fact that when this defendant was arrested, the story was given a great deal of publicity and it seems to me only fair to see that her exoneration should also be accompanied by a reasonable amount of publicity."

Judge Albert took his position in front of the scales and beckoned to Virginia to come and stand at his side.

Mason escorted the nervous defendant up to a position beside the judge.

"Come on and get in this picture, Mason," Judge Albert invited.

"I think I'd better not," Mason said. "That will make the picture look posed and artificial and it may not be in the best taste from the standpoint of legal ethics; but the picture

32

of you 'weighing the evidence' will attract a lot of attention."

Judge Albert nodded, said to Virginia, "Now, Miss Baxter, if you'll just look at the beam on the scales here, I'll bend over and be adjusting it— No, no, don't look at the camera, look at the scales. Turn a little if you want to so you can get your best angle for the camera."

Judge Albert put a hand on her shoulder, bent over and moved the balancing weight back and forth on the beam, and gleeful photographers exploded flash bulbs in rapid succession.

Judge Albert straightened, looked at Mason, then beckoned to the district attorney and led the two attorneys out of earshot of the reporters.

"There's something very fishy about this case," Judge Albert said. "I would suggest, Mr. Caswell, that you check very carefully on the person who gave you this information, or rather misinformation, which resulted in a search of that suitcase."

The prosecutor said hotly, "That person has always been on the up-and-up with us; his information has been reliable."

"Well, it wasn't reliable in this case," Judge Albert said.

"I'm not so certain about that," Caswell retorted. "After all, it's not entirely impossible that the bags could have been tampered with."

"I think they were," Judge Albert said bitingly, "but *I* think the tampering occurred after the bag was checked by Miss Baxter and before it was taken off the revolving rack.

"After all, this Court wasn't born yesterday and after you see defendants coming and going, day in and day out, you have an opportunity to learn something about human nature. This young woman isn't a dope pusher."

"And after you've seen Perry Mason pull grandstand after grandstand," Caswell rejoined, "you learn something about dramatics. This scene the Court has just participated in is going to give aid and comfort to a lot of persons who don't wish law enforcement any good."

"Law enforcement had better become more efficient then," Judge Albert snapped. "There was no objection to calling photographers to photograph this young woman when her suitcase was opened, and heaven knows how much harm was done her at that time. I only hope there will be enough publicity in connection with the events of the last hour to more than offset the unfavorable publicity which was given her at the time of her arrest."

"Well, don't worry," Caswell said bitterly, "this picture will go out over the wire services and make about a third of the papers in the United States."

"Let's hope it does," Judge Albert said, and turning on his heel, headed for chambers.

Caswell walked away without a word to Mason.

Mason rejoined Virginia Baxter. "Want to go in the witness room where we can sit down and talk for a minute?" Mason asked.

"Anything," she said. "Anything, Mr. Mason."

"I just want a word with you," Mason said.

He led her into the witness room, held a chair for her, sat down opposite her and said, "Now look, who would have it in for you?"

"You mean to try and frame me on a narcotics charge?"

"Yes."

"Heavens, I don't know."

"Your husband?"

"He was very bitter."

"Why?"

"I wouldn't give him a divorce."

"Why not?"

"He was a sneak, a liar and a cheat. He was carrying on with another woman all the time I was working my head off trying to help us get ahead.

"He even dipped into the joint account we had in order

to help finance a car for this woman; then he had the unmitigated gall to tell me that people couldn't control their emotions, that a man would fall in love and he'd fall out of love and there was nothing that could be done about it."

"How long ago was this?"

"About a year."

"And you didn't give him his freedom?"

"No."

"You're still married?"

"Yes."

"How long since you've seen him?"

"Not since that big blowup, but he has called me up on the phone once or twice and asked if I had changed my mind."

"And why haven't you changed your mind?" Mason asked.

"Because I'm not going to let them play fast and loose with me that way."

Mason said, "All right, you're going to remain married to him. What advantage will that be to you?"

"It won't be any advantage to me but it will keep them from taking advantage of me."

"In other words, anything that will be a detriment to the pair of them will be to your advantage. Is that the way you feel?"

"Well, something like that."

Mason regarded her steadily. "Is that the way you want to feel?"

"I . . . I just wanted to gouge her eyes out. I wanted to hurt her in every way I could."

Mason shook his head. "There's no percentage in that, Virginia. Ring him up and tell him that you've decided to let him have a divorce, that you'll file the divorce action—there's nothing in your religion against it, is there?"

"No."

"No children?"

"No."

Mason spread his hands in a little gesture. "There you are," he said. "You have a future, too, you know."

"I . . . I—"

"Meaning you've met someone in whom you're interested?" Mason asked.

"I . . . I have met lots of people and, for the most part, I have been plenty sour on men."

"But lately you've met one who seems to be different?"

She laughed nervously. "Must you cross-examine me now?" she asked.

Mason said, "Whenever you've made a mistake in life, the best thing to do is to wipe the slate clean and put that mistake behind you.

"However, what I wanted to talk to you about was the fact that someone is trying to put you in a position where you'll be discredited.

"I don't know who it is, but it's some person who has a certain amount of ingenuity and, apparently, some underworld connections.

"That person has struck once. You've avoided the trap, but other traps can be set and that person can strike again. I don't like it and if there's any possibility it's your husband, I'd like to eliminate him from the picture.

"There is, of course, the woman with whom your husband was in love and with whom, I presume, he is now living.

"Do you know her? Do you know anything about her background?"

"Not a thing. I know her name and that's just about all. My husband was very careful that I didn't learn too much about her."

"All right," Mason said, "here's my suggestion. File for a divorce on the ground of desertion or cruelty. Leave her name out of it, get it over with and get your freedom; and if there is anything out of the ordinary that happens within

36

the next few days, anything suspicious, any anonymous telephone calls, anything that seems strange, call me immediately."

Mason patted her shoulder and said, "You're free now."

"But what do I do about your fee, Mr. Mason?"

Mason said, "Send me a check for a hundred dollars when you get around to it and find it convenient, but don't worry about it."

Chapter 7

There had been a dearth of news the night before and as a result the story about "weighing" the evidence had been given considerable prominence.

Virginia Baxter read the papers with a growing sense of relief. The reporters had sensed that she had been framed and had done their best to see that her vindication was featured as top news.

The newspaper photographers, thoroughgoing professionals, had done an excellent job with their cameras, while Judge Albert, leaning over the scales, had placed a steadying and paternal hand on Virginia's shoulder.

It has been truthfully said that one picture tells more than ten thousand words, and in this case, the jurist's attitude left no doubt of his faith in Virginia Baxter's innocence.

The headlines in one of the newspapers read, FORMER LEGAL SECRETARY VINDICATED IN DOPE CASE.

One article made much of the fact that she had formerly been employed in a law office. While that office had in reality done little trial work, specializing in estate matters, the reporter had taken poetic license and had written that while Virginia Baxter had been working on criminal cases which Delano Bannock was defending, it probably had never occurred to her in even her wildest dreams that the time would come when she herself would stand before the bar of justice accused of a serious crime.

It was from an article in another evening paper that Virginia received a shock.

The reporter had done some background investigation

and the article stated that Colton Baxter, estranged husband of Virginia Baxter, was, by coincidence, an employee of the very airline which had checked the suitcase to its destination. He was not immediately available for comment.

Virginia read that twice, then impulsively reached for the telephone and called Mason's office. Suddenly, realizing the hour, she was about to hang up when, to her surprise, she heard Della Street's voice on the line.

"Oh, I'm so sorry. I didn't realize how late it was. This is Virginia Baxter. I read something in the paper that startled me and . . . I never thought about it being so long after five."

"Do you want to talk with Mr. Mason?" Della Street asked. "Just a minute and I'll connect you. I think he wants to talk with you, too."

A moment later, Mason's voice said, "Hello, Virginia. I suppose you've read the papers and learned that your husband was located by one of the reporters."

"Yes, yes, Mr. Mason. That makes it just as clear as day. Don't you see what happened? Colton planted that stuff in my suitcase and then tipped off the newspapers. If I had been convicted, he could then have had perfect grounds for divorce. He'd claim that I had been a dope fiend all the time we were married; that I had been dealing in dope and that he had left me because of that."

"So," Mason said, "what do you want to do?"

"I want to have him arrested."

"You can't arrest him without proof," Mason said. "All you have so far is surmise."

"How much would it cost to get proof?"

"You'd have to employ a private detective and he'd charge you probably a minimum of fifty dollars a day and expenses, and then the chances are he'd be unable to get anything except more grounds for surmise."

"I have a little money. I'd . . . I'd spend it in order to catch him—"

"Not through me, you wouldn't," Mason interrupted. "As a client of mine I wouldn't let you spend that amount of money for that purpose. Even if you got some evidence it would only leave you exactly where you are now, with good grounds for divorce.

"Why don't you just wash your hands of that man; get rid of him, dissolve the marriage and begin all over again.

"If you had religious reasons for not getting a divorce, I would probably handle it in another way, but you're going to get a divorce sooner or later and—"

"I don't want to give him that satisfaction."

"Why?"

"That's what he's wanted all along, a divorce."

Mason said, "You're not doing yourself a particle of good. All you're doing is some real or fancied harm to your husband. For all you know you may be playing into his hands right now."

"What do you mean?"

"He's playing around with this other woman," Mason said. "He keeps telling her that if he could ever get a divorce he'd marry her, but you won't give him a divorce. The woman knows all this is true.

"But suppose you give him a divorce, then he's in a position where he is not only free to marry this woman, but he has to do it to make good on his promises. He may not really want to marry her.

"It may be that your husband is in exactly the position he wants to be in."

"I had never thought of it that way," she said slowly, but then added quickly, "Then why did he plant the dope in my suitcase?"

"If he did, it was probably because he wanted to have you thoroughly discredited," Mason said. "Yours was one of those marriages that has been dissolved in hatred. You'd better quit looking back over your shoulder, turn around and face the future."

40

"Well, I— I'll sleep on it and let you know in the morning."

"Do that," Mason said.

"I'm sorry I disturbed you at this hour."

"Not at all. We were working on some briefs here in the office, and after I read that statement in the paper, I thought you might be calling, so I told Della to plug in an outside line.

"You're in the clear now, stop worrying."

"Thank you," she said, and hung up.

The phone had hardly been cradled when there was a buzz at the door of her apartment.

Virginia crossed over and opened the door a few inches.

The man who stood in the doorway was somewhere around forty-five years of age, with dark wavy hair, a close-clipped mustache and intense obsidian black eyes.

"You're Mrs. Baxter?" he asked.

"Yes."

"I'm very sorry to bother you at this time, Mrs. Baxter. I know how you must be feeling, but I come to you on a matter of some importance."

"What is it?" she asked, still keeping the chain on the door.

"My name," he told her, "is George Menard— I read about you in the paper. I don't like to bring up a disagreeable subject, but of course you know that the news of your trial has been in all the papers."

"Well?" she asked.

"I noticed in the paper that you had been the secretary of Delano Bannock, an attorney, during his lifetime."

"That's right."

"Mr. Bannock died several years ago, I believe."

"That also is correct."

"I am trying to find out what was done with his files," the man said.

"Why?"

"Frankly, I want to locate a paper."

"What sort of a paper?"

"A carbon copy of an agreement which Mr. Bannock drew up for me. I've lost the original and I don't want the other party to the agreement to know it. There are certain things that I have to do under that agreement and while I think I can remember what they are, it would be an enormous help if I could locate a carbon copy."

She shook her head. "I'm afraid I can't help you."

"You were employed by him at the time of his death?"

"Yes."

"What happened to the office furniture and all that?"

"Why, the office was closed up. There was no reason for the estate to go on paying rent."

"But what happened to the office furniture?"

"I believe it was sold."

The man frowned. "To whom was it sold? You know who bought the desks, filing cases, chairs?"

"No, they were sold to some second-hand office furniture outfit. I kept the typewriter I had been using. Everything else was sold."

"Filing cases and everything?"

"Everything."

"What happened to the old papers?"

"They were destroyed— No, wait a minute, wait a minute. I remember talking with his brother and telling him that the papers should be kept. I remember now, I wanted him to keep the filing cases intact."

"The brother?"

"That's right. Julian Bannock. He was the sole heir. There weren't any other relatives. The estate was a small one.

"You see, Delano Bannock was one of those devoted attorneys who was more interested in doing a job than in getting a fee. He worked literally day and night. He had no wife or family and he spent four or five evenings a week

42

in his office, working until ten or eleven o'clock. But the modern idea of keeping track of time by the hour just never occurred to him. He would put in hours and hours on some little agreement that had a point that interested him and then he'd make only a moderate charge. The result was that he didn't leave much of an estate."

"What about the fees that were due him at the time of his death?"

"I wouldn't know about that, but it's very well known that the estates of professional men have a lot of trouble with outstanding accounts."

"And where could I find Julian Bannock?"

"I don't know," she said.

"Do you know where he lived?"

"Someplace in the San Joaquin Valley, I think."

"Could you find out where?"

"I *might* be able to."

Virginia Baxter had been sizing up the man and finally unlatched the door chain. "Won't you come in?" she invited. "I think perhaps I can consult an old diary. I have been keeping diaries for years—" She laughed nervously— "not the romantic type, you understand, but business diaries that contain little comments about when I went to work at a certain place and how long I worked there, events of the day, when I received raises in salary and things of that sort.

"I know that I made some entries at the time of Mr. Bannock's death—oh, wait a minute, I remember now, Julian Bannock lived near Bakersfield."

"Do you know if he still lives there?"

"No, I don't. I remember now that he came down driving a pickup. The files were loaded into the pickup. I remember that after the files were loaded, I felt that my responsibility was ended. I turned the keys over to the brother."

"Bakersfield?" Menard said.

"That's right. Now, if you can tell me something about

43

your agreement, perhaps I can remember about it. Mr. Bannock had a one-man office and I did all of the typing."

"It was an agreement with a man named Smith," Menard said.

"What was the nature of the agreement?"

"Oh, it involved a lot of complicated things about the sale of a machine shop. You see, I'm interested, or was interested, in machinery and thought for a while I'd go into the machinery business, but— Well, it's a long story."

"What are you doing now?" she asked.

Menard's eyes suddenly shifted. "I'm sort of free-lancing," he said. "Buying and selling."

"Real estate?" she asked.

"Oh, anything," he said.

"You live here in the city?"

He laughed, obviously ill at ease. "I keep going from place to place—you know how it is when a person is looking for bargains."

Virginia said, "I see. Well, I'm sorry I can't help you any more than I have."

She stood up and moved toward the door.

Menard accepted the dismissal.

"Thank you so much," he said, and walked out.

Virginia watched him to the elevator then, when the door of the cage had slid shut, took to the stairs and raced down them.

She was in time to see him jump into a dark-colored car which had been parked in the only vacant parking space at the curb, a space directly beside a fireplug.

She tried to get the license number but was unable to get it all, because of the speed with which the driver whipped out into the street and drove away.

Her eyes focused on a distinctive zero as the first of the numbers and she had a somewhat vague impression that the last figure of the license was a two.

The car, she thought, was an Oldsmobile, perhaps two to

four years old, but here again she couldn't be certain. The man gunned the car into speed and drove away fast.

Virginia returned to her apartment, went into her bedroom, pulled out a suitcase, started rummaging through her diaries. She found the address of Julian Bannock in Bakersfield, an R.F.D. box and a notation in parentheses, "No telephone."

Then her phone rang. A woman said, "I found your name in the telephone directory. I just wanted to call you to tell you how glad I am that you beat that horrible frame-up."

"Thank you very much," Virginia said.

"I'm a stranger to you," the woman went on, "but I wanted you to know how I felt."

Within the next hour there were five more calls, including one from a man who was obviously drunk and certainly offensive, and another from a woman who wanted a willing ear to hear about *her* case.

Finally, Virginia ignored the telephone, which continued to ring until she went out to dinner.

The next morning she asked the telephone company to change her number and give her an unlisted one.

Chapter 8

Virginia found she couldn't entirely get the matter of those papers off her mind.

After all, Julian Bannock had been a rancher. He and his brother had not been particularly close, and Julian was interested only in liquidating everything in the estate and getting rid of it just as rapidly as possible.

Virginia knew there had been many important probate proceedings and agreements, but after she had turned the key over to Julian Bannock, she had paid no more attention to the estate.

But the thought of those files left her vaguely uneasy, and there had been a false note about George Menard. He had seemed all right until she had asked him about himself, then he had suddenly become evasive. She felt sure he had been lying about his background.

After all, she felt something of a responsibility for those files.

She called Information to try to place a call to Julian Bannock at Bakersfield and was informed he still had no telephone.

She tried to forget the matter and couldn't. Suppose Menard was up to something tricky.

She wanted to find out about his car registration but didn't know how to go about it without consulting Perry Mason, and she felt she had bothered him too much already.

She determined to drive out to Bakersfield and talk things over with Julian Bannock.

She left at daylight, made inquiries at Bakersfield, and found that Julian Bannock lived some ten miles out of the city.

She located his mailbox, drove in for some three hundred yards, came to a yard with a barn, several sheds, a house, shade trees and a variety of farming implements—tractors, cultivators, hayrakes, disks—stored more or less haphazardly in the yard.

A dog ran barking to the car, and Julian Bannock came out.

Despite the fact she had only seen him in his "dressed up" clothes, she recognized him instantly in his coveralls and work shirt.

"Hello!" he said.

"Hello, Mr. Bannock. Remember me? I'm Virginia Baxter. I was your brother's secretary."

"Oh, yes," he said, his voice cordial. "Sure. I knew I'd seen you before somewhere. Well, come on in. We'll fix you up a breakfast, eggs from our own yard, and maybe you'd like some homemade bread and preserves—fruit right off our own trees here."

"That would be wonderful," she said, "but I wanted to talk with you about a few things."

"What?"

"Those papers that you took," she said. "Those filing cases. Where do you have them?"

He grinned at her. "Oh, I sold all those quite a while ago."

"Not the files?"

"Well, I told the fellow to take everything. The stuff was cluttering up a lot of room here and— You know what? Mice were getting in those papers. They'd get up in there and start chewing on the papers to make nests."

"But what actually became of the *papers*? Did the man who bought the files—"

"Oh, the papers! No, they're here. The man who bought

47

the filing cases wouldn't take the papers. He dumped them all out. He said the papers made the files too heavy to carry."

"And you burned them up?"

"No, I tied them up in bundles with binder twine. I guess the mice are getting in there pretty bad—you know the way it is around a ranch, you have a barn and mice live in the barn.

"We've got a couple of cats now that have been keeping things down pretty well, but—"

"Would it be all right to take a look?" she said. "I'd just like to see about some of the old papers."

"Funny thing," he said, "that you'd be worrying about those. There was a fellow here yesterday."

"There was?"

"That's right."

"A man about forty-five?" she asked. "With very intense black eyes and a small stubby mustache? He wanted—"

Julian Bannock interrupted her by shaking his head. "No," he said, "this was a fellow around fifty-five but he had bluish sort of eyes and was sort of light-complected.

"This fellow's name was Smith. He wanted to find some agreement or other."

"And what did you do?"

"I told him where the papers were, told him to look around and help himself if he wanted. I was busy and he seemed a mighty nice fellow."

"Did he find what he wanted?"

Julian Bannock shook his head. "He said that things were too much of a mess for him to unscramble. He said he didn't know anything about the files. If he could get hold of the key to the filing system, he thought he could maybe find the paper he wanted.

"He asked me if I knew anything about how the files were classified and I told him I didn't."

"It was all handled according to numbers," Virginia said.

"General classifications. For instance, number one to a thousand was personal correspondence. Number one thousand to three thousand represented contracts. Three thousand to five thousand, probate. Five thousand to six thousand, wills. Six thousand to eight thousand, agreements. Eight thousand to ten thousand, real estate transactions."

"Well, I didn't disturb anything. I put all that stuff in packages and tied them up with binder twine."

"Could we take a look?" Virginia asked.

"Why, sure."

Julian Bannock led the way into the relative coolness of the barn, redolent with the clean smell of hay.

"Used to keep this barn pretty full of hay," he said, "and had quite a storage problem. Lately, I've been selling the hay because I haven't been doing much feeding. Used to have a little dairy business, but they've got so many headaches now that the small dairyman has too much of a problem; too much work; too many regulations.

"The real big dairies are handling things now with mechanical milkers, feeders and all that sort of thing— I didn't get too much for those filing cases, either. Could have kept the stuff in the cases, I guess, but I don't know what anybody'd want with all that stuff—thought some of pitching it all out and burning it up, but you talked so much about the files, I thought I'd keep them."

"Well, of course, that was some time ago," Virginia said. "As time passes, those files cease to have quite as much importance."

"Well, here we are, over here. This used to be a tractor shed, but I got room to put these— Well, *what* do you know!"

Bannock stopped in surprise before the litter of papers strewn all over the floor.

"Looks like that fellow left a hell of a mess," he said angrily.

Virginia looked in dismay at the piles of paper.

The man who had been in there had evidently cut the binder twine that had held the papers in different classifications and had pawed through everything looking for the paper he wanted, throwing the other papers helter-skelter into a pile which had spread out into an area some six feet in diameter at the bottom and some four feet high.

Virginia, looking at the carbon copies now ragged at the edges from the gnawing of mice, thinking of the care she had taken with those papers when she had typed them, felt like crying.

Julian Bannock, slow to anger, but with a steadily mounting temper, said, "Well, by gosh, I'd like to tell that fellow Smith a thing or two!"

He bent down and picked up a piece of binder twine. "Cut through slick and clean with a sharp knife," he said. "Somebody'd ought to take that man and teach him a few manners."

Virginia, studying the pile of papers, said, "He must have been in a terrific hurry. He was looking for something and he didn't have time to untie the twine, look at each package, and then tie them up again. He simply took his knife, cut the twine, looked hurriedly for what he wanted; then when he didn't find it, he threw the rest of the papers over on the pile."

Julian said thoughtfully, "You can see that all right. I'm kicking myself for not keeping an eye on him."

"How long was he here?" Virginia asked.

"Now, that I can't tell you. I let him in the barn, showed him where the things were and then left."

Virginia reached a sudden decision. "Where is the nearest telephone?" she asked.

"Well, one of the neighbors has one and he's real accommodating," Julian said. "He lives about two miles down the road."

"I want to make a long distance call," she said, "and . . . I guess it's better not to let anyone hear what I'm saying.

I'll go on in to Bakersfield and put in the call from a booth there. I'll be back after a while with some big cartons. I'm going to put those papers in the cartons and then we'll keep them someplace where they're safe."

"Okay," he said, "I'll give you a hand when it comes to putting them in. Do you think I should stack them up now and—"

"No," she said, "there's still some semblance of order. A good many of the classifications are still segregated. Somewhere there's a master book which gives the numbers and an index. That is, it was here.

"If you don't mind, I'd like to stop at one of the supermarkets and get some big cartons; then come back and try and put this stuff together again so it makes some sort of sense."

"Well, now," he said, "if you want to do it, that's fine with me, but it's a lot of work to go through and it's pretty dusty in here. You're all dressed up neat as a pin and—"

"Don't worry," she said, "I'm going to get some blue jeans and a blouse in town. If you don't mind, I'll change my clothes when I get back and get to work."

"Sure thing," he said, "we'll give you a place to change in the house, and a chance to take a bath when you're finished. This is going to be pretty dusty."

"I know it is," she said, laughing, "but us ranchers have to get used to a little dust now and then."

He grinned at her, thrust out his hand and shook hands.

"You're all right," he announced.

Virginia returned to her car, drove to Bakersfield and called Perry Mason, just as the lawyer was reaching his office.

"You wanted me to tell you if anything unusual happened," she said, "and this is unusual enough, but I just can't understand the significance."

"Go ahead," Mason said, "tell me what it is."

"You'll probably laugh and think my imagination is

working overtime. There's probably no way on earth it can be connected with anything but— Well, here's what happened."

She told him about Bannock, the papers, about the man who had called on her, his description and a general but somewhat vague description of the automobile in which he had driven away. "A model about two to four years old, I would guess. I think it was an Oldsmobile," she said. "The first figure of the license number was a zero. I tried to get it but he drove away very fast."

"Where was he parked?" Mason asked. "Could you see the parking place from which he drove his car? That might tell us how long he'd been waiting. I presume parking places right in front of your apartment house are hard to find."

"I'll say they are!" she exclaimed. "But this man didn't have any trouble. He parked right in front of the fireplug."

"Then he hadn't been there very long," Mason said. "That means he must have followed you home rather than been there waiting. I would think the police would check that fireplug space rather often."

"They do! I had a friend who parked just long enough to leave a parcel, yet she got a parking ticket. It wasn't over a minute."

"You think the first number on the license plate was a zero?" Mason asked.

"Yes, I'm quite certain of that, and I *think* the last number was a two, but I'm not at all certain of that."

"You're in Bakersfield now?" Mason asked.

"Yes. I went out to Mr. Bannock's brother's place to check with him and found that someone had been out there; gone through all the files."

"What do you mean by 'going through them'?" Mason asked.

She described the files.

Mason's voice became crisp with authority.

"Now, this is important, Virginia. You say the files were all cut open?"

"Yes."

"Every single bundle?"

"Yes."

"And their contents spread out?"

"Yes."

"No single bundle was intact?"

"No."

"You're sure of that?"

"Why, yes. Why is it important, Mr. Mason?"

"Because," Mason said, "it indicates a strong probability that the person who is searching didn't find what he was looking for.

"In other words, if you're looking for a particular paper and you're in a hurry, you cut open bundle after bundle of papers until you find the one you want; then you shove it in your pocket and get away from there fast. That would leave some bundles that hadn't been cut open.

"But if, on the other hand, *all* of the bundles are cut open, it's a pretty good indication that the person didn't find what he was looking for."

"I never thought of that," she said.

"You're going back to Julian Bannock's?"

"Yes, I'm taking some cardboard cartons and am going back and I'll try to make some semblance of order out of those files."

"All right," Mason said, "by the time you get back there, we'll find out something about your man who is interested in the files. . . . Now, tell me, Virginia, what about wills?"

"What do you mean?"

"When Bannock would prepare a will it would usually be executed there in the office?"

"Yes."

"Who would be the subscribing witnesses?"

"Oh, I see what you mean. He would usually sign as one

53

of the subscribing witnesses and I would sign as the other witness."

"And you had a classification of various wills? In other words, you had a file number designating wills that you had executed in the office?"

"Oh, yes, I see what you mean now. Files numbered five thousand to six thousand were wills."

"All right," Mason said, "when you go back, take a look at the five to six thousand 'will' file. See how intact it is. Tie that file up and bring it here just as fast as you can make it."

"Why that file in particular?" she asked.

Mason said, "Bannock has been dead for a few years. Most of the agreements and things that he had drawn would no longer be important, but if some relative wanted to find out what was in a certain will—"

"I get you," she interrupted excitedly. "Why didn't *I* think of that. Of course, that's what it is."

"Don't jump to conclusions," Mason warned. "This is just a thought, but I think we'd better take precautions."

"I'm going right back," she promised, "and I'll keep that file of wills with me. I'll leave the other papers for a later trip."

Mason said, "If anything else happens that is in any way out of the ordinary, give me a ring. In the meantime, I'm going to find out something about this visitor of yours."

Virginia promised to report anything new that happened, hung up the telephone, went to a supermarket, secured two cartons and then returned to Julian Bannock's place.

She found Bannock apprehensive.

"What's the matter?" she asked. "Did something else happen about those files?"

"You hadn't been gone five minutes," he said, "when a fellow showed up here who fitted the description you had given me of the man you thought was here. He was in his late forties or early fifties, had a mustache and eyes that

54

were so dark you couldn't see any expression in them. It was like looking at a pair of black, polished stones."

"That was the man all right," she said. "What did he want?"

"Said *his* name was Smith, and he asked about my brother's files."

"What did you do?"

"I told him that we weren't letting people look at those files. He said it was important and I told him that he could sit right here and wait; that my brother's secretary was going to be here in an hour or so and that he could wait for her."

"What happened?"

"That gave him a jolt—knowing that you were coming here. He said he couldn't wait."

"Were you able to get his license number?" she asked eagerly.

"No, I wasn't," Julian said, "because he'd plastered mud all over it. There's a place up here where irrigating water sometimes runs over the road and there was quite a puddle up there that he'd gone through, but it wasn't mud that would cover a license number. I think he'd got out and deliberately plastered mud on the license."

"Well," Virginia said, "I'm going to get at those files, tie them up again and I think I'd better take some of them with me, if you have no objection."

"Take them all if you want," he said. "I can't be here all the time and if there's anything important in those papers, people could sneak in while I'm out in the fields someplace and get hold of them."

She asked, "Have you ever heard of Perry Mason, the attorney?"

"I'll say I have. I've read a lot about him."

"Well," Virginia said, "he's my lawyer. He's advising me, and I'm going to get in touch with him and do exactly as he says.

"I was going to clean up all these files and put them in boxes, but I don't have time now. I'm just grabbing this file with these numbers—let's look around and see if there are any more of these files here that have numbers between five thousand and six thousand."

Virginia scooped up a number of filing jackets that were all together and had numbers between five and six thousand. Then she and Julian made a hasty search for any other papers numbered within those brackets.

"They seem to have been all together in that bunch," Julian said.

"All right," Virginia told him. "Now, I'm going to rush these in to Mr. Mason's office. I want to get in there before lunch, if possible. Will you do the best you can to see that these others aren't disturbed while I'm gone?"

"You want me to put them in boxes?" Julian asked. "I'm sort of busy this time of year, what with irrigation and—"

"No," she said, "just leave them the way they are, if you can. But put a lock on the door—you know, a padlock. Try to keep anyone from coming in the barn.

"If anyone should try to get in, be sure to get his license number and make him give you proof of his identity. Ask to see his driving license."

"Will do," Julian said, grinning. "You don't want to go in the house and change into jeans and blouse?"

"No, there isn't time. I'm on my way. I hope I didn't get too dusty. Goodbye."

"Goodbye, ma'am," he said, and then added, "I know how much my brother thought of you and I guess he sure was a good judge of character."

She flashed him a smile, jumped in her car, placed the carton with the five-to-six thousand classification in the back seat, and took off.

Chapter 9

It was shortly after noon when Virginia reached Perry Mason's office.

Gertie, the receptionist, said, "Hello, Miss Baxter, they're expecting you, but I'd better give them a buzz and let them know you're here."

Gertie buzzed the phone, and a moment later Della Street came out and said, "Right this way, Virginia. We have some news for you."

Virginia followed Della Street into Mason's private office to find the lawyer frowning thoughtfully. "We've traced your mysterious visitor, Virginia," Mason said. "The one who gave you the name of George Menard. We traced him through his parking at the fireplug. We went through all the parking tickets issued by the officer who patrols that district. There were three fireplug parking tickets. One of them was for a license number ODT 062. That car is registered to a man whose description is very similar to that of the man who called on you."

"Who is he?"

"His real name is George Eagan, and he is employed as a chauffeur for Lauretta Trent. So we did a little checking and—"

"Lauretta Trent?" Virginia exclaimed.

"You know her?" Mason asked.

"Why, we did some legal work for her and— Why, yes, I'm quite certain we made at least one will for her. I have rather a vague memory that it was an unusual will. The relatives were given rather small amounts, all things considered, and there was an outsider who got the bulk of the estate. It may have been a nurse—or a doctor. Heavens! It *could* have been the chauffeur!"

Mason said, "We've found out some rather interesting things."

"About the chauffeur?"

"About Lauretta Trent. She has recently had three attacks of so-called food poisoning. The hospital records describe them as gastroenteric upsets."

Virginia said, "I've got all the old copies of wills locked in my car down in the parking lot, Mr. Mason, if it would help any. . . ."

"It will help a lot," Mason said. "I'm going to introduce you to Paul Drake, our detective. He handles all our investigative work; he's head of the Drake Detective Agency, which is on this floor— Give him a ring, will you please, Della?"

Della Street asked Gertie for an outside line. Her fingers flew over the dial. After a moment, she said, "Paul, Della. Perry would like to have you come to the office right away, if you can."

Della smiled and hung up. "He'll be here within a matter of seconds."

And it was only a matter of seconds before Paul Drake's code knock sounded on the door.

Della opened the door and let him in.

"Paul," Mason said, "this is Virginia Baxter. You probably don't know it but she's the client whom I've been representing and is the reason you have been doing this investigative work."

"I see," Drake said, smiling at Virginia. "Pleased to meet you, Miss Baxter."

Mason said, "She has some papers locked in her car down in the parking lot. Could you help her bring them up?"

"How heavy?" Drake asked. "Do I need anyone to help me?"

"Oh, no," she said, "it's a bundle of papers probably twenty inches thick. But one man can lift them."

"Let's go," Drake said.

"There's one more thing I wanted to tell you, Mr. Mason," Virginia said. "While I was away from Julian Bannock's ranch, or farm, or whatever you call it, and telephoning you and getting ready to go back and get those papers, this man showed up at the ranch."

"What man?"

"The one who called on me. Eagan, you say he is, the chauffeur for Mrs. Trent."

"And what did he want?"

"He wanted to look at some of the old files of Delano Bannock. Julian—that's the brother—told him to wait, that I was going to be back there within a few minutes."

"And what happened?"

"The man jumped in his car and drove off, going fast."

"I see," Mason said, and nodded to Drake. "Let's get those papers, Paul."

Drake accompanied Virginia to the parking lot. She unlocked her car. Drake picked up the files in the cardboard carton, hoisted the carton to his shoulder and they returned to Mason's office.

Mason said, "Let's look at the files listed under 'T' and see what you have. Let's see, you have 'T-1,' 'T-2,' 'T-3,' 'T-4,' 'T-5'; just what do those mean?"

"That's the way I kept the wills under 'T.' 'T-1' would be the first five letters of the alphabet. In other words, 'T-A,' 'T-B,' 'T-C,' 'T-D,' 'T-E'; then 'T-2' would be the next five letters."

"I see," Mason said. "Well, let's look under the 'T-4' and see if we can find any papers relating to Lauretta Trent."

Mason spread the files out on the desk and he, Della

59

Street, Paul Drake and Virginia Baxter started rapidly going through them.

"Well," Mason said, after a few minutes' search, "apparently we have a lot of copies of wills here, but no copy of a will made for Lauretta Trent."

"But we did her work, we made at least one will for her," Virginia said.

"And," Mason said, "George Eagan was making inquiries as to the location of the carbon copies of Delano Bannock's files, and George Eagan is Lauretta Trent's chauffeur."

Mason turned to Paul Drake. "What hospital was Lauretta Trent in when she had her so-called digestive upsets?"

"Phillips Memorial Hospital," Drake said.

Mason nodded to the phone. "Get them on the line, please, Della."

Della Street asked for an outside line, got a number and whirled the dial. A moment later she nodded to Mason.

Mason picked up the phone. "Phillips Memorial Hospital?" he asked.

"Yes."

"This is Perry Mason, the attorney," the lawyer said. "I would like to get some information on one of your patients."

"I'm sorry, we can't give information about our patients."

"Well, this is just a routine matter of record," Mason said casually. "The patient is Lauretta Trent. You had her in the hospital on three occasions within the last several months and all I'm interested in is finding out the name of her physician."

"Just a moment, we can give you that information."

"I'll hold the phone, if I may," Mason said.

A moment later the voice said, "The physician was Dr. Ferris Alton. He's in the Randwell Building."

"Thank you," Mason said.

The lawyer hung up, turned to Della Street, "Let's see if we can get Dr. Alton's nurse."

"His nurse?"

"Yes," Mason said, "I'd like to talk with Dr. Alton, but I think I'll have to speak with his nurse, personally, before we can get him on the line. After all, this is probably the beginning of a busy afternoon for a doctor. He probably sees a lot of office patients in the afternoon, does operating in the morning and makes hospital visits after that."

Della Street got the number, asked Gertie in the outer office for an outside line, dialed the number and again nodded to Perry Mason.

Mason picked up the telephone, said, "How do you do? This is Perry Mason, an attorney. I know that Dr. Alton is very busy and that this is just before the busiest time of the afternoon, but it is quite important that I speak with him briefly concerning a matter which may affect a patient of his."

"*Perry* Mason, the lawyer?" the feminine voice asked.

"That's right."

"Oh, I'm quite sure he'd want to talk with you personally. He's busy at the moment, but I'll interrupt him and— Can you hang on to the line for a few moments?"

"I'll be glad to," Mason said.

There was a period of silence. Then a tired, slightly impatient voice said, "Yes, this is Dr. Ferris Alton talking."

"Perry Mason, the attorney," the lawyer told him. "I wanted to ask you a few questions about a patient of yours."

"What sort of questions, and who is the patient?"

"Lauretta Trent," Mason said. "You've had her hospitalized several times within the last few months."

"Well?" Dr. Alton asked, and this time the note of impatience was quite apparent in his voice.

"Can you tell me the nature of the malady?"

"I can not!" Dr. Alton snapped.

"Very well, then," Mason said. "I can perhaps tell you something which will be of interest. I have reason to believe that Lauretta Trent made a will; that this will was executed in the office of an attorney by the name of Delano Bannock; that the attorney is now deceased; that persons are interested in surreptitiously obtaining a copy of that will; that some of the persons associated with Lauretta Trent may be taking an active interest in a search of this kind.

"Now then, I am asking you this. Are you completely satisfied with your diagnosis in the case of Lauretta Trent?"

"Certainly. Otherwise I wouldn't have discharged her."

"I understand, generally," Mason said, "that she had a gastroenteric disturbance."

"Well, what of it?"

"And," Mason said, "I have before me several of the authorities on forensic medicine and toxicology. I find that it is generally agreed that cases of arsenic poisoning are seldom diagnosed by the attending physician, since the symptoms are those of a gastroenteric disturbance."

"You're crazy," Dr. Alton said.

"Therefore," Mason went on, "I think you will understand my position when I ask you if there were abdominal cramps, cramps in the calves of the legs, a burning sensation in the stomach and—"

"Good God!" Dr. Alton interrupted.

Mason ceased talking, waiting for the doctor to say something.

There was a long period of silence over the phone.

"No one would possibly want to poison Lauretta Trent," Dr. Alton said.

"How do *you* know?" Mason asked.

There was another period of silence.

"What's your interest in this matter?" Dr. Alton asked at length.

"My interest is purely incidental," Mason said. "I can assure you that while I am representing a client, that client has no interests adverse to those of Lauretta Trent and there is no reason why you could not make any statement to me that you can make without disclosing a privileged professional confidence."

Dr. Alton said, "You've given me something to think about, all right, Mason. Her symptoms had a great deal in common with those of arsenic poisoning. You're *so* right, physicians who are called in on cases of this sort almost never suspect the possibilities of homicidal poisoning. The cases are almost invariably given a diagnosis of enteric disturbance."

"That," the lawyer told him, "is why I'm calling you."

"Do you have some suggestions?" Dr. Alton asked.

"Yes," Mason said. "I would suggest that you get a sample of her hair pulled out by the roots, if possible. And, if possible, some cuttings of the fingernails. Let's have them analyzed for arsenic and see if we get a positive reaction.

"In the meantime, I would suggest that you try not to alarm your patient, but take steps to see that she is put upon a restricted diet which is enforced by special round-the-clock nurses—in other words, a rigid dietary supervision.

"I take it the patient is in such a financial position that the expense can be justified?"

"Of course," Dr. Alton said. ". . . My Lord, she has a heart condition which can't stand too many of these upsets. I warned her, the last one. I thought it was dietary indiscretion. She has a weakness for highly spiced Mexican food with considerable garlic— That would be almost a perfect disguise for a dose of arsenic— Mason, how long are you going to be in your office?"

"I'll be here all afternoon," Mason said, "and if you need me after office hours, you can get me through the Drake Detective Agency. Ask for Paul Drake. The offices are in the same building where I have my offices and are on the same floor."

"You'll be hearing from me," Dr. Alton said. "In the meantime, I'm going to make arrangements right away to insure that nothing else questionable will happen."

"Please bear in mind that we must try to keep from making any accusations or any statements which will alarm your patient until we're certain," Mason said.

"I understand, I understand," Alton said sharply. "Damn it, Mason, I've been practicing medicine for thirty-five years— My God, man, you've given me a jolt. . . . Classic symptoms of arsenic poisoning and I never suspected a thing—you'll be hearing from me. Goodbye."

The connection was sharply terminated.

Mason said to Virginia, "I don't like to restrict your liberties, Virginia, but I want you to be where I can reach you. Go to your apartment and stay there. Report every single thing out of the ordinary. I'll have my phone so you can get to me at any time."

Drake frowned and said, "But they couldn't prove a will by using a copy, could they, Perry?"

"Under certain limited circumstances, yes," Mason said. "If a will is missing, the general presumption is that it was destroyed by the testator, which is equivalent to a revocation. But if, for instance, a house should catch on fire and the testator should perish in the flames, it would be generally presumed that the will was burned up at the same time and, if there could be proof that it was still in effect at the time of the fire and the testator's death, then the contents could be established by secondary evidence.

"However, that's not what I'm thinking of."

"What are you thinking of?" Drake asked.

Mason glanced at Virginia and shook his head. "I'm not prepared to say at the moment.

"Virginia, I want you to go on home. You may receive a call from this man you now know is George Eagan, Lauretta Trent's chauffeur.

"You'll remember this man told you he was George Menard.

"Now, if he calls on you, be very careful not to let on that you know who he really is. Be naïve, gullible and perhaps a little greedy. If he acts as if he wanted to make you any sort of a proposition, let him feel you are willing to listen. Then stall for time.

"Call me—or if I'm not available, Paul Drake—as soon as you can get to a phone. Let us know what the man wants."

"I'm to let him think I'm willing to play along?"

"That's right. And if you are asked to do any typing, use new carbons with each sheet of paper."

"It won't be dangerous?"

"I don't think so at the moment. Not if you don't let on you know who he really is, and if you manage to stall him long enough to get to a phone. Later on we may have to take precautions."

"All right," she promised, "I'll try."

"Good girl," Mason said. "Go on home now and phone me if anything happens."

Her laugh was nervous. "Don't worry," she said, "the very first thing that occurs out of the ordinary, I'm going to dash to a telephone."

"That's right," Mason told her. "Get Paul Drake on the line if you can't get me. His office is open twenty-four hours a day."

Della Street held the exit door open for her.

"Just be careful," Mason warned, "not to let this chauffeur know that you have any idea who he is. Be naïve, but let him feel that if he has any proposition to make you could be tempted."

Virginia Baxter flashed him a smile and left the office.

Della Street gently closed the door.

"You think this chauffeur is going to be back?" Drake asked.

65

"If he didn't ge what he wanted," Mason said, "he'll be back. We have two people looking for a paper, and since the paper that we *think* they're looking for doesn't seem to be in the files, the probabilities are that one of them has already found it. Therefore, the other will be back."

"Just how significant is all of this?" Drake asked.

"I'll tell you," Mason said, "when we get the samples of hair and fingernails from Lauretta Trent. A person can't rely on a copy of the will unless two things have happened."

"What two things?" Drake asked.

"First, the original will is missing. Second, the person who executed it is lead."

"You think it's that serious?" Drake asked.

"I think it's that serious," Mason said, "but my hands are tied until we get a check on that arsenic factor.

"Go back to your office, Paul, alert your telephone operator and have things in readiness so that you can have a man out at Virginia Baxter's place at a moment's notice."

Chapter 10

The man with the black hair, the close-clipped mustache and the black, intense eyes was waiting in a car that was parked in front of Virginia Baxter's apartment house.

Virginia spotted the car first, recognized the driver sitting there concentrating on the front door of the apartment house and breezed on by without attracting any attention.

From a service station four blocks down the street, she telephoned Mason's office.

"He's out there, waiting," she said, when she had the lawyer on the line.

"The same man who called on you before?" Mason asked.

"Yes."

"All right," Mason said, "go on home; see what he wants; make an excuse to break away if you can and call me."

"Will do," she said. "You'll probably hear from me within the next twenty or thirty minutes."

She hung up the phone, drove back to her apartment house, parked her car and entered the front door, apparently completely oblivious of the man who was seated in the parked automobile across the street.

Within a matter of minutes after she had entered her apartment house, the buzzer sounded.

She saw to it that the safety chain was on the door, then opened it to confront the intense, black eyes.

"Why, hello, Mr. Menard," she said. "Did you find what you wanted?"

The man tried to make his smile affable. "I'd like to talk with you about it. May I come in?"

She hesitated a brief instant, then said cordially, "Why, certainly," and released the chain on the door.

He entered the apartment, seated himself, said, "I'm going to put my cards on the table."

She raised her eyebrows.

"I wasn't looking for an agreement made with Smith and relating to the sale of a machine shop," he said. "I was looking for something else."

"Can you tell me what?" she asked.

"Some years ago," he said, "Mr. Bannock made at least one will for Lauretta Trent. I'm under the impression he made two wills.

"Now then, for reasons that I don't want to take the time to go into at the present time, it is highly important that we find those wills. At least, the latest one."

Virginia let her face show surprise. "But—but I don't understand. . . . Why, we only had the carbon copies. Mrs. Trent would have the original wills in her safety deposit box or somewhere."

"Not necessarily," he said.

"But what good would a copy do?"

"There are other people who are interested."

She raised her eyebrows again.

"There is one person in particular who is willing to do anything to get his hands on a copy of the will. Now, I would like to lay a trap for that individual."

"How?"

"I believe you purchased the typewriter that you had used in the office?"

"Yes. That is, Mr. Bannock's brother gave it to me."

He indicated the typewriter on the desk. "It's an older model?"

"Yes. We had it in the office for years. It's an exceedingly durable make and this model is pretty well dated.

When the appraiser appraised the office furniture he put a very low value on this typewriter because it was so old, and Mr. Bannock's brother told me to just keep it and forget about it."

"Then you could prepare a carbon copy of a will and date it back three or four years and we could mix that carbon copy in with the old papers that went to Mr. Bannock's brother and if anyone should happen to be snooping around through those papers looking for a copy of Lauretta Trent's will, we could fool him into relying on that copy and perhaps get him to betray himself."

"Would that do any good?" she asked.

"It might do a great deal of good. . . . I take it you'd like to help a person who was a client of Mr. Bannock's?"

Her face lit up. "Then you mean Lauretta Trent would ask me to do this herself?"

"No, there are certain reasons why Lauretta Trent couldn't request you to do it, but I can tell you it would be very much to her advantage."

"You're connected with her then in some way?"

"I am speaking for her."

"Would it be all right for me to ask the nature of the association or of your representation?"

He smiled and shook his head. "Under some circumstances," he said, "money talks."

He took a wallet from his pocket and extracted a hundred-dollar bill. He paused for a moment; then extracted another hundred-dollar bill. Then, significantly, another hundred-dollar bill and kept on until there were five one-hundred-dollar bills lying on the table.

She eyed the money thoughtfully. "We'd have to be rather careful," she said. "You know Mr. Bannock used stationery that had his name printed in the lower left-hand corner."

"I hadn't realized that," the man said.

"Fortunately, I have some of that stationery— Of course,

69

we'd have to destroy the original and leave this as a carbon copy."

"I think you could make a good job of it," he said.

She said, "I'd have to have your assurance that it was all right, that there wasn't going to be anything fraudulent connected with it."

"Oh, certainly," he said. "It's simply to trap someone who is trying to make trouble with Mrs. Trent's relatives."

She hesitated for a moment. "Could I have some time to think this over?"

"I'm afraid not, Mrs. Baxter. We're working against time and if you're going to go ahead with this we'd have to do it immediately."

"What do you mean by 'immediately'?"

"Right now," he said, indicating the typewriter.

"What do you want in this will?"

He said, "You make the usual statements about the testatrix being of sound and disposing mind and memory and state that she is a widow; that she has no children; that she has two sisters who are married; that one is Dianne, the wife of Boring Briggs; that the other is Maxine who is the wife of Gordon Kelvin.

"Then go on and state that you have recently become convinced that your relatives are actuated by selfish interests and that, therefore, you leave your sister Dianne a hundred thousand dollars; that you leave your sister Maxine one hundred thousand dollars; that you leave your brother-in-law Boring Briggs ten thousand dollars; that you leave your brother-in-law Gordon Kelvin ten thousand dollars; that you leave your faithful and devoted chauffeur, George Eagan, who has been loyal to you throughout the years, all of the rest, residue and remainder of your estate."

Virginia Baxter said, "But I don't see what good that is going to do."

"Then," her visitor went on firmly, "you make another will which purports to have been executed just a few weeks

70

before the date of Mr. Bannock's death. In that will you state that you leave Maxine and Gordon Kelvin one thousand dollars apiece; that you leave Boring Briggs and his wife Dianne one thousand dollars apiece, being satisfied that these people are actuated purely by selfish interests and have no real affection for you, and you leave all the rest, residue and remainder of the estate to your faithful and devoted chauffeur, George Eagan."

She started to say something, but he held up his hand and stopped her.

"We will plant those copies of the spurious wills in with Mr. Bannock's papers.

"I can assure you that they will be discovered by persons who are trying to find out in advance the terms of Lauretta Trent's will.

"These two documents will show that some years ago she began to doubt the sincerity of her sisters and particularly her brothers-in-law; that more recently she uncovered proof that they were simply trying to get what they could get their hands on and were actuated by purely selfish motives."

"But, don't you understand," she said, "that neither of these wills would be any good at all if— Well, I always signed and witnessed wills that were executed in the office. Mr. Bannock signed, and I signed.

"If they should call me and ask me if I signed this will as a witness, I would have to tell them that this will was completely spurious; that I prepared it only recently and—"

He interrupted her, smiling. "Why don't you just leave all that to me, Mrs. Baxter?" he asked. "Just pick up the five hundred dollars and start typing."

"I'm afraid I'd be too nervous to do anything while you were here. I'd have to work out the terms of the wills and then you could come back later."

He shook his head firmly. "I want to take these documents with me," he said, "and I haven't very much time."

Virginia Baxter hesitated, then remembering Mason's instructions, went to the drawer of the desk, picked out some of the old legal paper bearing Delano Bannock's imprint, put in new carbon paper, racheted the paper into the typewriter and started typing.

Thirty minutes later, when she had finished, her visitor pocketed the carbon copies of the two documents, said, "Now, destroy those originals, Virginia. In fact, I'll destroy them right now."

He picked up all the originals and copies, folded them and put them in his pocket.

He walked to the door, paused to nod to Virginia Baxter. "You're a good girl," he said.

She watched him until he had entered the elevator; then she slammed the door, raced for the telephone, called Mason's office and hurriedly reported what had happened.

"Do you have any copies?" Mason asked.

"Only the carbon paper," she said. "He was smart enough to take the originals as well as the copies, but I followed your suggestion and put in a fresh sheet of carbon paper with each page and he didn't notice what I was doing. You see, I prepared all the pages with the carbon paper inserts in advance, putting out a half a dozen pages on my desk at one time and taking a fresh sheet of carbon paper from the box for each page. So I have a set of carbons, and by holding them up to the light, it's easy to read what was written."

"All right," Mason said, "bring those carbon copies up to my office just as fast as you can get here."

Chapter 11

Virginia sat across the desk from Mason, who carefully examined the pages of carbon.

He turned to Della Street. "Della," he said, "take some cardboard the size of these pages of carbon paper so the carbon paper won't get folded or wrinkled, put these in an envelope and seal the envelope."

When Della had done this, Mason said to Virginia, "Now, write your name several times across the seal."

"What's that for?"

"To show that it hasn't been steamed open or tampered with."

Mason watched her while she wrote her name.

"Now then," he said, "don't bother with your car because you won't be able to find a parking place and time is running against you.

"Take a taxicab. Rush this envelope to the post office, address it to yourself and send it by registered mail."

"Then what?" she asked.

"Now, listen very carefully," Mason said. "When this envelope is delivered to you by registered mail, don't open it. Leave it sealed just as it is."

"Oh, I see," she said, "you want to be able to show the date that I—"

"Exactly," Mason said.

She picked up the envelope, started for the door.

"How are you fixed for provisions in your apartment?" Mason asked.

"Why, I . . . I have butter, bread, canned goods and some meat. . . ."

"Enough to last you for twenty-four hours if necessary?"

"Yes, indeed!"

Mason said, "Mail that letter, go back to your apartment, stay there, keep the safety chain on the door. Don't admit anyone. If anyone calls to see you, tell him that you're entertaining a visitor and can't be disturbed. Then get his name and telephone me."

"Why?" she asked. "Do you think I'm in . . . in any danger?"

"I don't know," Mason said. "All I know is that there's a possibility. Someone tried to frame you and discredit you. I don't want that to happen again."

"Neither do I," she said vehemently.

"All right," Mason told her. "On your way to the post office. Then go back to your apartment and stay there."

When she had left, Della Street looked at Mason with raised eyebrows. "Why should *she* be in any danger?"

Mason said, "Figure it out for yourself. A will is made. There are two subscribing witnesses. One of them is dead. An attempt was made to put the other in a position where her testimony would have been discredited. Now, a new plan is in operation."

"But those spurious wills; they can't mean anything."

"How do you know?" Mason asked. "Suppose two more people die, then what happens?"

"What two people?" she asked.

"Lauretta Trent and Virginia Baxter. Perhaps a fire destroys the home of Lauretta Trent. Presumably the will has been destroyed in the conflagration.

"People look for the carbon copies of the wills prepared by Bannock to establish the contents of the burnt will. They find two wills. The effect of those wills is to indicate that Lauretta Trent was suspicious of her relatives and the people who surrounded her.

"Now then, Delano Bannock is dead. Suppose Virginia Baxter should also die."

Della Street blinked her eyes rapidly. "Good heavens . . . are you going to notify the police?"

"Not yet," Mason said, "but probably within a matter of hours. However, there are a lot of factors involved, and an attorney can't go around making accusations of this sort unless he has something more definite on which to base them."

"But it won't take much more?" Della Street asked.

"It will take very little more," Mason said.

Chapter 12

It was just before Mason was closing the office that Dr. Alton telephoned.

"Is it all right if I come up for just a few minutes?" Dr. Alton asked. "I've had a terrific workload this afternoon with an office full of patients and I'm just this minute getting free."

"I'll wait," Mason said.

"I'll be there within ten minutes," Dr. Alton promised.

Mason hung up the phone, turned to Della Street. "Any particular plans for this evening, Della? Can you wait with me for Dr. Alton?"

"I'll be glad to," she said.

"After that," Mason told her, "we can go out for dinner."

"Now, those words are music to a secretary's ears," she told him, "but may I remind you, you don't as yet have any retainer in this case which would cover expenses."

"We're casting bread on the waters," Mason said, "and don't let the matter of expense cramp your style. Just don't look at the right side of the menu."

"My figure," she sighed.

"Perfect," Mason said.

She smiled. "I'll go out in the outer office and wait for Dr. Alton."

"Bring him right in, as soon as he comes," Mason told her.

Della Street went to the outer office and a few minutes later returned, opening the door and saying, "Dr. Ferris Alton."

Dr. Alton came bustling forward, radiating intense nervous energy.

He grasped Mason's hand, said, "I'm very pleased indeed to meet you, Mr. Mason. I have to discuss this case with you, personally, which is the reason I'm bothering you.

"Incidentally, I have here two sterile phials containing the material you wanted, some clippings from the fingernails and some hair that has been pulled out by the roots.

"Now, either I can have this processed or you can."

"Better let me do it," Mason said. "It will attract less attention that way, and I have some connections which will give me a report within a very short time."

"Well, I'd be very glad to have you do it," Dr. Alton said, "but now that you've planted the suspicion in my mind, I have an uneasy feeling that we're going to have positive reactions; that there will be at least two areas in the hair that will show arsenic.

"The first attack took place approximately seven and a half months ago—too long a time, I'd guess, for any traces of the poison to remain. But the second was five weeks ago, and the last one about a week ago."

"Did you get a dietary history?" Mason asked.

"I wasn't utterly naïve," Dr. Alton said. "I wanted to find out if this was the result of an allergy or, as I suspected, contaminated food.

"On all occasions, she had eaten Mexican food."

"Who cooked it?" Mason asked.

"She has a chauffeur, a George Eagan, who has been with her for some time. She is very much attached to him—in a business way, of course. He is young enough—Well, I believe there's quite a discrepancy in ages . . . oh, say fifteen years or so.

"He drives her everyplace and he is the one in charge of the outdoor cooking; whenever they have a barbecue, he does the steaks and the potatoes, does the cooking and the serving, toasts the French bread and all the rest of it. I gather he's very expert.

"He's also expert in cooking; the Mexican foods I mentioned are cooked out of doors."

"Wait a minute," Mason said, "she would hardly have the Mexican food cooked just for herself. There must have been others present."

Dr. Alton said, "In getting a case history, I wasn't even suspicious of poisoning. Therefore, I asked only about what my patient had been eating. I didn't ask about others. I believe other relatives were also present. Eagan, the chauffeur, did the cooking. Apparently no one else besides Lauretta Trent had any symptoms."

"I see," Mason said.

"If it was poisoning, and I am now satisfied it was, it was done very expertly. . . . Now then, Mr. Mason, I have a responsibility to my patient. I want to keep from having any recurrence."

"I told you what to do," Mason said sharply. "Get three nurses, put them on the job around the clock."

Dr. Alton shook his head. "I am afraid that won't work."

"Why not?" Mason asked.

Dr. Alton said, "We're not dealing with a child, Mr. Mason. We're dealing with a mature woman who likes to have her own way; who is rather arbitrary and—damn it, I've got to have some sort of an excuse to put out special dishes for her."

Mason's mouth tightened. "How many nurses are on the job now?"

"Just one . . . a nurse she has from time to time."

"And how did you get the fingernails and the hair?"

Dr. Alton said, uncomfortably, "I had to use a little subterfuge. I rang up the nurse and told her that I was going to give Mrs. Trent some medicine which might cause a temporary itching of the skin; that it was highly important that she not do any scratching and that I would like to have her nails trimmed down; that I wished she'd explain to the patient what I had in mind and what I was trying to accomplish. I also told her that I'd like to test the hair to see whether her digestive upsets had been due to an allergy caused by either a shampoo or a hair dye. I explained to the nurse that I didn't want to suggest that Mrs. Trent was coloring her hair; but that I felt there might be an allergy, particularly if she had had any itching or sore spots in her scalp and had scratched and had thereby caused an abrasion in the skin that would enable the dye materials to penetrate the bloodstream. I told the nurse to put the nail clippings and the hair in sterile phials."

Mason said, "Nurses take courses in poisons and their treatment. Do you think your nurse suspected anything?"

"Oh no, not a thing," Dr. Alton said. "I told the nurse I'd been puzzled about Mrs. Trent's case; that I couldn't believe that the disturbance resulted entirely from food poisoning but that I thought perhaps it might be a combination of things."

"She didn't give any indication that she thought your requests were unusual?" Mason asked.

"None whatever. She accepted them just as any good nurse would, without any comment. I told her to get a taxi and send the nail parings and the hair in their sterile phials to my office at once."

Mason said, "I know a laboratory which specializes in forensic medicine and toxicology that will give us a quick report on these, not a quantitative analysis, but it will show whether any arsenic is present."

"How soon can you have that?"

Mason said, "I think I can have it right after dinner, Doctor."

"I wish you'd telephone me," Dr. Alton said.

"All right," Mason told him, "but what have you done about furnishing your patient with round-the-clock protection?"

Dr. Alton's eyes shifted. "All right, Mason," he said, "I'll put it right on the line. You almost convinced me when you talked over the telephone, and then I became more convinced when I thought over the symptoms. But when I took time to think things over, I felt I couldn't justify taking really drastic steps pending a laboratory report; but I have taken precautionary steps which will be ample for the time being."

"What steps?" Mason asked, his voice coldly disapproving.

"I've decided that during the next few hours there won't be any element of real danger, particularly in view of the fact that this nurse, Anna Fritch, is on the job. However, I told her to see that Mrs. Trent was on a very bland diet tonight; that I intended to perform some tests and I wanted her to have nothing except soft boiled eggs and toast tonight; that I wanted the nurse to prepare both the eggs and the toast, and see that the eggs were served in the shell so that there would be no chance of too many spices being added."

"All right," Mason said, "if that's what you've done, that's what you've done. Give me your night number. I'll drop these things at the laboratory and ask for an immediate check. . . . Now, what do you propose to do if the tests are positive and show the presence of arsenic?"

This time Dr. Alton met Mason's eyes firmly. "I intend to go to the patient and tell her that she has been suffering from arsenic poisoning rather than from allergies or a digestive upset. I intend to tell her that we're going to have to take extraordinary safeguards and that, from the manner in which the symptoms developed, I have very strong suspicions that there was an attempt at homicide."

Mason said, "And I suppose you have taken into consideration that this will start a three-ring circus among relatives, authorities and people in the household. They'll call

80

you a quack, an alarmist and accuse you of trying to alienate Lauretta Trent's affections."

"I can't help it. I have my duty as a doctor."

"All right," Mason said. "We should have that report no later than nine-thirty. The only thing that I don't agree with you on is safeguarding your patient in the meantime."

"I know, I know," Dr. Alton said. "I've debated the pros and cons with myself and I have come to the conclusion that this is the best way to handle it. I'll accept responsibility for the decision. After all, you know, it is *my* responsibility."

Mason nodded to Della Street. "All right, Della, we'll go to the laboratory, start them working on these things, and get a preliminary report at the earliest possible moment. You get Dr. Alton's night number and we'll call him just as soon as we have a report."

"And, of course," Dr. Alton said, "you'll keep things entirely confidential? You know, the police and, of course, the press. These things have a way of leaking out once they get into the hands of the police, and I know that Lauretta Trent would consider publicity—well, she'd simply hit the ceiling. It would mean the end of our professional relationship."

Mason said, "I'm in somewhat the position of being a public servant in this case, Doctor. Actually, I haven't a client. The logical client would probably be Lauretta Trent, but I certainly don't want to approach her in any way."

"You don't have to," Dr. Alton said. "The minute you find anything positive in the hair and the nails, I'm going to go to her myself and I'm going to explain to her just what you have done in the case and how valuable your assistance has been.

"In the meantime, I can assure you, on my own responsibility, that any amounts within reason you may be called upon to pay will be promptly remitted by Mrs. Trent.

"But . . ." Dr. Alton cleared his throat, "in the event your suspicions should turn out to be groundless, Mr. Mason, you are— Well, I . . . I mean to say—"

Mason grinned and interrupted him. "You mean that in the event I'm barking up the wrong tree, my costs are going to be borne exclusively by me; that I will have lost a lot of face with you."

Dr. Alton said, "You've expressed it more forcefully than I would, but very well."

Mason said, "You'll hear from me about nine or nine-thirty and then you can take it from there."

"Thank you," Dr. Alton said.

He gripped the lawyer's hand and went out.

Della Street looked at Mason speculatively. "Do you have some mental reservations about Dr. Alton?" she asked.

Mason said, "Do you know, Della, I can't help feeling what a mess it would be if Dr. Alton should be one of the beneficiaries in Lauretta Trent's will."

Della Street's eyes widened with consternation. "Good heavens," she said, "do you suppose . . . ?"

"Exactly," Mason said as her voice trailed away into silence. "And now, let's go to dinner, after stopping by the laboratory and asking for a quick preliminary report."

"And you're going to tell Dr. Alton what you find? If he's one of the beneficiaries under the will— Well, of course, under the circumstances—"

"I know," Mason said, "I'm going to tell him and then I'm going to make absolutely certain that Lauretta Trent is protected against any further so-called gastroenteric disturbances."

"That," Della Street said, "should make quite a situation."

"It will," Mason told her.

Chapter 13

Mason and Della Street had a leisurely, relaxing dinner.

Della Street had left word with the laboratory to call them at the café, and the headwaiter, knowing that an important call was expected, was bustling about keeping an eye on Mason's table.

Della Street had contented herself with a small steak and baked potato, but Mason had ordered an extra-thick cut of rare prime ribs of beef, a large bottle of Guinness stout, tossed salad and stuffed baked potato.

At length, the lawyer pushed back his plate, finished the last of his stout, smiled across the glass at Della Street and said, "It's a real pleasure to be able to dine, to feel that we're not wasting time and yet be able to take all the time we want.

"We have the laboratory doing our analysis for us; we have Paul Drake all ready to— Oh-oh," the lawyer interrupted himself, "here comes Pierre with a telephone."

The headwaiter bustled importantly to the table, conscious of the fact that many eyes were on him as he plugged in the telephone for his distinguished guest.

"Your call, Mr. Mason," he said.

Mason picked up the telephone, said, "Mason talking."

The operator said, "Just a moment, Mr. Mason." And then Mason heard a quick, "On the line."

"Mason talking," the lawyer said.

The voice of the laboratory technician was almost mechanical as he rasped out a report.

"You wanted an analysis of nails and hair for arsenic. Both reactions were positive."

"Quantity?" Mason asked.

"It was not a quantitative analysis. I simply ran tests. However, I can state this: There are two bands of arsenic in the hair indicating a recurrent poisoning with a lapse of about four weeks in between the attacks. The nails do not give that long a sequence but do indicate the presence of arsenic."

"Can you make an analysis which would give me an idea of the quantity?" Mason asked.

"Not with the material which I have at present. I gathered that haste was imperative and I used up the material in making tests simply for the purpose of getting a reaction to the poison."

"That's fine," Mason said, "thanks a lot, just keep it under your hat."

"Anything to report to the authorities?"

"Nothing," Mason said positively. "Absolutely nothing."

The lawyer hung up the phone, scribbled the amount of a tip on a check which the headwaiter had brought him; signed his name and handed the headwaiter ten dollars.

"This is for you, Pierre. Thanks."

"Oh, thank you so much," Pierre said. "The call it was all right? It came through nicely?"

"It came through fine," Mason said.

The lawyer nodded to Della Street. They walked out of the restaurant, and Mason stopped at the telephone booth to deposit a coin and dial Dr. Alton's night number.

Mason heard the phone start ringing, and almost instantly Dr. Alton's voice said, "Yes, yes. Hello. Hello," indicating that the physician had been anxiously waiting by the telephone.

"Perry Mason talking, Doctor," the lawyer said. "The tests were both positive. The hair test indicated there had

84

been two periods of poison ingestion about four weeks apart."

There was a long moment of stunned silence at the other end of the telephone; then Dr. Alton said, "Good God!"

Mason said, "She's *your* patient, Doctor."

Dr. Alton said, "Look, Mason, I have reason to believe that I am named as one of the beneficiaries in Lauretta Trent's will.

"This whole business is going to put me in a very embarrassing position. As soon as I make a report to Lauretta Trent, I will be castigated by the family who will insist on calling in another physician to check my diagnosis and then when that physician confirms our suspicions, the family will at least intimate that I have been trying to hurry up my inheritance."

Mason said, "You might also give a little thought to what will happen if you *don't* report what you have found out and if there should be a fourth attack during which Mrs. Trent should die."

"I've been pacing the floor thinking of that for the last hour," Dr. Alton said. "I knew that you disapproved of the extent of the precautionary measures I had taken. You thought that I should at least have confided my suspicions to the nurse in charge and seen that— Oh, well, that's all water under the bridge now.

"Mason, I'm going out there. I'd like very, very much to have you along with me when I talk with my patient. I think I'm going to need professional reinforcements and before I get done, I may need an attorney. I want to have you there to substantiate the facts. I'll see that you're amply paid by Mrs. Trent. I'll make that my responsibility."

"What's the address?" Mason asked.

"An imposing mansion on Alicia Drive, the number is twenty-one twelve. I'm going right out there. If I should get there first, I'll wait for you. If you get there, just park your car at the curb on the street and wait for me.

"Actually, there's a curved driveway going up to the front entrance, but the only place you could wait without attracting attention would be at the curb."

"All right," Mason told him. "Della Street, my secretary, and I are on the way out right now."

"I'll probably beat you there," Dr. Alton said. "I'll be parked at the curb."

"Any idea of just how you are going about it?" Mason asked.

Dr. Alton said, "I've been overly optimistic long enough. Perhaps I should say, I've been a coward."

"You're going to tell her the whole thing?"

"Tell her the whole thing. Tell her that her life is in danger. Tell her that I have made a mistake in diagnosis. In short, I'm going to set off the whole chain reaction."

"You know her," Mason asked, "how will she take it?"

"I don't know her that well," Dr. Alton said.

"Haven't you been treating her for quite a while?"

"I've been her physician for years," Dr. Alton said, "but I don't know her well enough to know how she'll take anything like this. No one does. She is very much of a law unto herself."

"Sounds interesting," Mason said.

"Probably interesting to you," Dr. Alton told him, "but it's disastrous as far as I'm concerned."

"Now, don't be too hard on yourself," Mason said. "Physicians don't ordinarily expect homicidal poisoning, and the records show that virtually every case of arsenical poisoning was originally diagnosed by the physician in charge as a gastroenteric disturbance of considerable magnitude."

"I know. I know," Dr. Alton said. "You can make it easy on me, but I'm not going to. I'm going to face the music."

"All right," Mason told him, "I'll meet you there."

The lawyer hung up; nodded to Della Street.

"Report to Paul Drake, Della. We're going out there. We can't let Dr. Alton face the music alone."

Chapter 14

Mason found Alicia Drive without difficulty; drove slowly along until the street lights showed an imposing white mansion on high ground to the right with a curved driveway leading up to the front.

A car was parked at the curb just before the entrance to the driveway and the parking lights were on. A figure could be seen silhouetted in the driver's seat.

Mason said, "Unless I'm mistaken, that will be Dr. Alton."

The lawyer eased his car into the curb behind the other machine, and Dr. Alton almost instantly opened the door of his car and came walking back to Mason's side of the car.

"Well," Dr. Alton said, "you made good time. Let's go."

"Take both cars in the driveway?" Mason asked.

"I think so. I'll lead the way; you follow me. There's a parking place in front. That is, it's wide enough for three cars and you just leave your car behind mine."

"Let's go," Mason told him.

Dr. Alton hesitated a moment, squared his shoulders, marched grimly over to his automobile, started the motor, switched on the headlights and led the way up the curving drive.

Mason followed behind him, parked his car, walked around to help Della out; then led her up the steps to the spacious stone landing.

Dr. Alton pressed the bell button.

Apparently Alton had expected a servant to open the

door. He recoiled noticeably when a chunky, blue-eyed man in his middle fifties stood in the doorway.

"Why, hello, Doc," the man said. And then added almost instantly, "What's the matter? Anything wrong?"

Dr. Alton said with dignity, "I happened to be driving by . . . I decided to drop in to see Mrs. Trent."

The man turned speculative blue eyes on Perry Mason and Della Street.

"And these people?" he asked.

Dr. Alton, evidently upset by the meeting, apparently did not intend to perform introductions.

"They are with me," he said shortly, and started through the door.

Mason took Della Street's arm, guided her into the reception hallway, smiled affably but impersonally and started to follow Dr. Alton up a sweeping staircase.

"Hey, wait a minute!" the man said. "Hey, what is this?"

Dr. Alton turned, frowned, reached a decision. "I have asked these people—"

"Why, this is Perry Mason, the lawyer!" the man interrupted. "I've seen his picture dozens of times."

Dr. Alton, with close-clipped professional efficiency, said, "Quite right. That is Mr. Perry Mason and, in case you're interested, the young woman with him is Miss Della Street, his secretary. I want Mr. Mason to talk with Mrs. Trent."

Then, after a barely perceptible hesitation, he said, "This is Mr. Boring Briggs, a brother-in-law of my patient."

Briggs didn't even acknowledge the introduction.

"Say, what is this?" he asked. "You folks making out a will or something? What's happened? Lauretta hasn't had another one of her spells, has she?"

Dr. Alton said, "I would prefer to let Mrs. Trent give you the information, but if it will relieve your mind any, Mr. Mason is with me. Mrs. Trent didn't send for him."

"Well, don't be so crusty about it," Briggs said. "I naturally felt a little alarm. I've been out. Just got back a few minutes ago, and when I find a doctor and a lawyer coming out to the house at this hour of the night—well, I felt I was entitled to a little information, that's all."

"We'll go on up," Dr. Alton said with formal dignity. "Right this way, please."

The physician indicated the stairway with a sweep of his arm and climbed the stairs.

Mason and Della Street followed a tread behind.

Briggs stood at the foot of the stairs and watched them go up, his expression one of frowning contemplation.

Dr. Alton reached the head of the stairs, started down the corridor with long strides. Then slowed perceptibly for a moment just before coming to a door where he knocked.

A woman opened the door.

This time Dr. Alton performed the introductions. "Miss Anna Fritch," he said. "Trained nurse.

"Miss Fritch, this is Miss Della Street, Perry Mason's secretary and Mr. Perry Mason, the attorney."

Her eyes widened. "Why, how do you do? How do you do?" she said.

Dr. Alton pushed his way into the room; held the door open for Della Street and Perry Mason. "How's the patient?" he asked.

The nurse's eyes met his. She lowered her voice and said, "She's gone."

Dr. Alton's face was apprehensive. "You mean she's—"

"No, no," the nurse hastened to explain, "she is out somewhere."

Dr. Alton frowned. "I told you to take precautions about her diet and—"

"Why, certainly," the nurse said, "I put it on the chart. She had dry toast which I fixed myself on an electric toaster and two soft-boiled eggs which I cracked myself. There was no seasoning at all. I'm afraid I may have gone to extremes. I insisted she eat the eggs without salt and I told her that you didn't want her to have any seasoning to-night."

"But you didn't tell her to stay in?"

"You didn't tell me to tell her that."

"Is she driving?"

"I think George Eagan, the chauffeur, is driving her."

"How long has she been gone?"

"I don't know. I didn't even know she was going. She didn't come out through here. There's an exit door from her bedroom to the corridor. You can see for yourself."

The nurse crossed the bedroom to an adjoining bedroom and opened the door.

It was a huge bedroom with rose tapestry, indirect lighting, a king-sized bed with a telephone beside it, half a dozen comfortable chairs, an open door to a bathroom and another door leading to the corridor.

"She didn't tell you she was going out?"

"I had no idea of it."

"What time did you give her the toast and eggs?"

"About seven o'clock, and I impressed on her that you didn't want her to have anything else."

"What did she say when you told her I suspected an allergy and wanted samples of her hair and her nails?"

"She was most co-operative. She said she certainly would like to find out what was causing the trouble, that somehow she didn't think her troubles were due to what she had eaten. She suspected some sort of an allergy."

Dr. Alton said, "It's important, very important that I see her— You don't know when she'll be back?"

The nurse shook her head.

"Nor when she went out?"

"No, Doctor, it's just as I told you. I looked in on her after she had had her supper and she was gone."

"She isn't in the house?"

"No, I asked and someone said she had taken the car and gone out."

90

Dr. Alton walked over to the bedroom and closed the door. Then he closed the corridor door and turned to Anna Fritch.

"Did you have any clue as to why I wanted hair and nail scrapings?" he asked.

Her eyes avoided his.

"Did you?" Dr. Alton asked.

"I wondered."

"Did you suspect?"

"The request, coupled with your instructions about diet— Well, I prepared the food myself and didn't let anyone else near it."

"Then you did suspect?"

"Frankly, yes."

The door from the corridor opened, and Boring Briggs, accompanied by another man, entered the room.

"I demand to know what's going on!" Briggs said.

Dr. Alton regarded the two men with cold disdain. "I am giving instructions to the nurse."

"And you need a lawyer with you for that?" Briggs asked.

Dr. Alton said to Mason, "Mr. Mason, meet the other brother-in-law, Gordon Kelvin."

Kelvin, a tall, distinguished-looking man in his late fifties, who gave the impression of being a frustrated actor, advanced a step, bowed slightly from the waist and extended a hand with great dignity. "Pleased to meet you, Mr. Mason," he said, and then added after a moment, "and may *I* ask what you're doing here?"

Mason said, "I came to see Mrs. Trent."

"This is rather an unusual hour for a call," Kelvin said.

Mason's smile was disarming. He said, "I have been able to order my life along unconventional patterns and no longer refrain from doing what I want to do simply because it is odd, unusual, distinctive or unconventional."

The lawyer beamed at the two irate brothers-in-law.

The men exchanged glances.

"This is no occasion for levity," Kelvin said.

"I am not being facetious. I am being accurate," Mason said.

Briggs faced Dr. Alton, "Will you," he asked, "once and for all, tell us the reason for this?"

Dr. Alton hesitated for a fraction of a second, then said, "Yes, I'll tell you the reason for it. I made a wrong diagnosis on Lauretta Trent's illness."

"You did!" Briggs exclaimed in surprise.

"That's right."

"A mistaken diagnosis?" Kelvin asked.

"Exactly."

"And you admit it?"

"Yes."

Again, the men exchanged glances.

"Would you kindly tell us the real nature of the illness?" Briggs asked.

"We want to know if it's ... serious," Kelvin supplemented.

"I dare say you do," Dr. Alton said dryly.

Briggs said, "Our wives have been out, but are expected back at any moment. They will perhaps be in a little more favorable position when it comes to ... well ... to getting information from you."

"Demanding an explanation," Kelvin supplemented.

"All right," Dr. Alton said angrily, "I'll give it to you. I made a mistake in diagnosis. I thought your sister-in-law was suffering from a gastroenteric disturbance induced by eating food that was tainted."

"And now you say that was not the correct diagnosis?" Briggs asked.

"No," Dr. Alton said. "It was not."

"What was the correct diagnosis?" Gordon Kelvin asked.

"Someone had deliberately given her arsenic trying to poison her," Dr. Alton said.

92

In the shocked silence that followed, two women came bustling into the room, two women who looked very much alike, women who spent much time and money in beauty shops and had evidently just been at one that day.

They were girdled so heavily they had an awkward stiffness of motion, their chins were held high and their hair was beautiful.

Dr. Alton said, "Mrs. Briggs and Mrs. Kelvin, Mr. Mason; and Miss Street, Mr. Mason's secretary."

Mrs. Kelvin, perhaps a few years older than her sister, but with keen inquisitive eyes, immediately took the initiative. "What's all this about?" she asked.

Boring Briggs said, "Dr. Alton has just told us he made a mistake in diagnosing Lauretta's illness, that it wasn't food poisoning at all; it was arsenic poisoning."

"Arsenic!" Mrs. Kelvin exclaimed.

"Bosh and nonsense!" Mrs. Briggs snapped.

"He seems certain," Gordon Kelvin said, "apparently—"

"Bosh and nonsense! If the man's made one mistake, he could make two. Personally, I think Lauretta needs another doctor."

Dr. Alton said dryly, "You might speak to Lauretta about it."

Boring Briggs said, "Now, look here, is all this going to get into the newspapers?"

"Not unless you let it get into the papers," Dr. Alton said.

"You're communicating with the police?"

"Not as yet," Mason said.

There was a moment's silence.

Mason went on calmly, "To a large extent, it's up to you folks. I take it this is a situation you wouldn't want to have publicized. I can also well realize that you have received the information with feelings of mingled emotion, but we are now facing facts, and one doesn't argue with facts."

"How do *you* know they are facts?" Briggs demanded.

Mason met his eyes and said coldly, "Laboratory facts. Positive evidence."

"You can't get evidence of something that's past that way," Briggs said.

Mason said, "Something that isn't generally known is that arsenic has an affinity for fingernails and hair. Once it gets in the system, it reaches the nails and the hair and lasts for a long, long time. Late this afternoon, Dr. Alton had samples taken of Lauretta Trent's hair and her fingernails. I, personally, had an analysis made by a laboratory that is highly competent.

"The answer was arsenic poisoning. In the hair, they were able to trace the intervals of arsenic poisoning.

"Now then, Dr. Alton is Lauretta Trent's personal physician. He's seen fit to disclose this information."

"Because," Dr. Alton said, "I'm trying to save the life of my patient. I think I have treated her long enough to understand something of her temperament. The minute I tell her that she has been a victim of arsenic poisoning, things are going to start happening around here."

"I'll say they are," Mrs. Briggs said. "Lauretta will hit the ceiling."

"One dose of arsenic poisoning," Dr. Alton went on, "may be more or less accidental; two doses indicate a deliberate attempt at homicide. Apparently, there have been three."

His announcement was greeted with silence.

After a moment, Mrs. Kelvin said, "These tests, are they absolute—that is, could there be any mistake?"

"They're absolute," Mason said. "There can be no mistake."

Mrs. Briggs said, "That first time she got sick was after she ate all that Spanish food. George cooked up the food on the grill in the patio."

"We all had it," Mrs. Kelvin said. "That is, the first time."

94

"And only Lauretta got sick," her husband pointed out.

Dr. Alton said, "Spanish food would be an ideal means of concealing an attempt at arsenic poisoning."

"That second time she got sick," Mrs. Briggs went on, "George had been doing some more outdoor cooking."

"Who is George?" Mason asked.

"George Eagan, the chauffeur," Gordon Kelvin said.

"And he doubles as a cook?" Mason asked.

"He doubles in almost anything and everything. He's with Lauretta most of the time."

"Too much of the time, if you ask me," Mrs. Kelvin snapped. "The man is positively trying to dominate her thinking."

Mason said, "Would you, by any chance, know whether he is remembered in her will?"

They exchanged shocked glances.

"Does anyone know the terms of her will?" Mason asked.

Again there were glances and a significant silence.

"Apparently," Mason said, "Delano Bannock was Lauretta Trent's attorney during his lifetime. Does anyone know if she has a will which was drawn in his office, or whether she went to some other attorney after Bannock's death?"

Kelvin said, "Lauretta jealously guards her private affairs. Perhaps she feels there is too much of her family living with her. She has become very secretive about all of her personal affairs."

"Financial affairs," Mrs. Briggs said.

"Both personal and financial," Mrs. Kelvin added.

Mason said, "I have reason to believe that the situation at the present time may be somewhat crucial."

"How did you get a sample of her hair and fingernails?" Kelvin asked.

"I instructed the nurse," Dr. Alton said.

Kelvin turned to Anna Fritch. "Did George Eagan know that you were taking samples of hair and nails?"

"She told him," Anna Fritch said. "She was bubbling over with enthusiasm that her illnesses might have been the result of an allergy. She seemed in very high spirits."

"An allergy?" Kelvin asked.

Dr. Alton said, "I explained to Nurse Fritch here that I wanted some tests made for an allergy, that there was a possibility the patient's symptoms might have been a violent and acute reaction to an allergy. I asked her to get samples of hair and nails and to explain to the patient that I was taking the nails because I was going to give her some medicine that would cause a skin irritation and I didn't want her to scratch. I also said that I thought the digestive upset she had had might have been due to an allergic reaction to a certain type of hairdressing—those things *do* happen, you know."

Kelvin said with dignity, "I think instead of standing here and becoming angry at Dr. Alton, we should give him our thanks and start doing something."

"Doing what?" Mrs. Briggs asked.

"Trying to locate Lauretta for one thing."

Mrs. Kelvin said, "She's out with that chauffeur of hers. Heaven knows where they've gone or when they'll be back. What are we going to do about trying to locate her? Call the police?"

Gordon Kelvin said, "Of course not. However, we know certain places where she might be. There are several restaurants that she frequents. There are a few friends on whom she might be calling. I would suggest that we get on the telephone and start calling, being very, very careful not to do anything which would indicate there might be any urgency in what we are trying to do."

"You two girls are probably the ones to do it. Start ringing her friends on the phone, say casually it's a little late to be calling, but that you want to speak with Lauretta.

"If it turns out Lauretta is there, take it in stride. Tell her that she's wanted home at once, that . . . that her sister isn't feeling at all well.

"Whichever sister happens to locate her can say it's the other sister who has been taken ill, and ask Lauretta to come home at once.

"In that way the chauffeur won't feel that we're suspicious of him and won't try to—well, won't try anything."

"Such as what?" Briggs asked.

"There are lots of things he could try," Mrs. Kelvin snapped.

"Well, we don't want him to get suspicious; we want him to walk right into our trap," Kelvin said.

"What trap?" Mason asked.

They looked at him for a moment, then Kelvin said, "He's the only one who could have poisoned her, don't you see?"

"No, I don't see," Mason said. "I can see grounds for suspicion but it's a long way from suspicion to actual proof. I would suggest that you be rather careful before you start talking about traps."

"I see your point," Kelvin said. "However, let's start trying to locate her and get her home. At least she'll be safe here."

"She hasn't been," Mason said.

"Well, she's going to be now!" Kelvin snapped.

"I agree with you," Dr. Alton said. "I am going to explain to her exactly what has happened; I am going to put my cards on the table, and I am going to see that she has private nurses around the clock, and that all food which she ingests is taken under the supervision of those nurses."

"Fair enough," Kelvin agreed. "I don't think anyone will object to that."

He turned to the others.

"Will they?" he asked.

Mrs. Briggs said, "Oh, stuff and nonsense! You can't put

her in a virtual prison that way, or an isolation ward or something; once Dr. Alton tells her, she can be on her guard. After all, she's old enough to live her own life. She doesn't need to be isolated from all her pleasures simply because Dr. Alton said someone has tried to poison her."

Dr. Alton said angrily, "You can shorten that sentence by leaving out the words 'Dr. Alton said' and have the sentence stand *'simply because someone tried to poison her.'* "

Mrs. Briggs said, "I am not accustomed to shortening my sentences."

Mason caught Dr. Alton's angry expression. "I think we'll be going, Doctor," he said.

"Well, I'm going to wait and see if they can get in touch with my patient," Dr. Alton said.

The telephone rang sharply.

"That's Lauretta calling now," Mrs. Kelvin said. "Answer it, Nurse, and then let me talk with her."

The nurse answered the phone.

"It's for Mr. Perry Mason," she said.

"Excuse me," Mason said to the others and took the phone. "Yes, hello," he said.

Virginia Baxter's voice came over the wire. "Mr. Mason, is it all right for me to see Lauretta Trent?" she asked.

Mason's eyes made a quick survey of the curious faces in the room.

"Where?" he asked.

"Up at a motel above Malibu."

"When?"

"She's overdue now. At first I thought it would be the thing to do, but after I got here I wasn't so certain."

"Where's here?"

"The motel."

"Where?"

"Here— Oh, I see what you mean. It's the Saint's Rest, and I'm in Unit Fourteen."

"Telephone there?"

"Yes. In each of the units."

"Thanks," Mason said, "I'll call back. Wait."

The lawyer hung up.

Mason nodded to Della Street, bowed to the gathering, said, "If you'll excuse us, please, we'll be going."

Dr. Alton said, "I may want to reach you later, Mr. Mason."

"Call the Drake Detective Agency," Mason said. "They're open twenty-four hours a day. They'll relay messages."

Mason started for the door.

Mrs. Briggs said, "Before you leave, Mr. Mason, I want you to know that we are absolutely horrified by what Dr. Alton has told us—and we are very much inclined to think there is more to it than appears on the surface."

Mason bowed. "You are, of course, entitled to your opinion. My only answer is to wish you a very good night."

The lawyer stood aside for Della to precede him through the door.

Chapter 15

Della Street said, "I take it that call must have been important since it caused you to leave the scene of conflict."

"That call," Mason said, "was from Virginia Baxter. Evidently, Lauretta Trent has been in touch with her and has arranged a meeting at a motel called the Saint's Rest, up in the Malibu country somewhere.

"The motel has a telephone and our client is in Unit Fourteen.

"So we call her back at the first available opportunity," Mason went on. "I'm looking for a booth now, but I want to get far enough away from Lauretta Trent's house so that some of the crusading brothers-in-law won't notice me in case they should start out on a search for Lauretta."

"What do you think is going on?" Della asked.

"I don't know," Mason said, "but quite obviously there's a tie-in between the wills that were prepared in Bannock's office and the attitude of the various potential heirs."

Della said, "It's pretty convenient for the chauffeur. He inherits under the will. He does all the outdoor cooking. Lauretta Trent likes highly spiced foods and every once in a while she has a violent digestive disturbance. Perhaps nothing which would be fatal in itself, but ... well, a violent nausea may bring on a fatal heart attack."

"Exactly," Mason commented.

"There's a service station and a phone booth down that side street," Della Street exclaimed. "I just had a glimpse of it as we drove by."

"That's for us," Mason said.

They made a U-turn, drove down the side street and into the service station.

Della entered the booth, called Information and got the number of the Saint's Rest Motel while Mason was giving instructions to the attendant to fill the car with gasoline.

Mason was just entering the phone booth when Della made the connection and asked for Unit 14.

She eased out of the booth while Mason stepped in past her and took the telephone from Della's hand.

"Hello, Virginia?" he asked when he heard his client's voice.

"Yes. Is this Mr. Mason?"

"Yes. Tell me what happened."

Virginia Baxter said, "I know that you told me to stay home, but the phone rang and it was Lauretta Trent. She asked me if I would mind meeting with her tonight to discuss a very important and very confidential matter. I told her that it would be inconvenient and that I was supposed to stay home.

"So she told me that she'd make it well worth my while. That she would pay all my expenses and give me five hundred dollars. But the understanding was I must refrain from communicating with *anyone*. Just go up there and wait for her."

"And you did?" Mason asked.

"I did. That five hundred dollars and all expenses looked as big to me as a mountain of pure gold.

"I realized I should have telephoned you but she specifically stated that I wasn't to get in touch with anyone. Not to let a single soul on earth know where I was."

"So?" Mason asked.

"So I came up here and I've been here for something over an hour and she hasn't shown up or sent me any message. I began to think about the fact that I'd let you down and so I decided to call you and tell you where I was.

"I called Paul Drake's office. They told me that you were

101

out at Lauretta Trent's so I called there and the nurse put you on the phone."

"You hold everything," Mason said. "We're on our way out to the Saint's Rest Motel. If Lauretta Trent shows up before we get there, hold her there."

"But how can I hold her?"

"Make some excuse," Mason said. "Tell her that you have some very important information for her. If you have to, tell her that I'm on my way out.

"Tell her that you want to talk with her privately. Tell her the whole story, starting with your arrest and all about the carbon copies of the files from Delano Bannock's office."

"You think my arrest was connected with that?"

"Very much so," Mason said. "I think the idea was that you were to be put in such a position that your testimony could be discredited if it became necessary to discredit it."

"All right," she said, "I'll wait."

"Where are you?"

"I'm in my room here at the motel."

"You've been there for how long?"

"More than an hour."

"And your car?"

"It's outside in the parking lot."

"All right," Mason said, "we're coming right out."

The lawyer hung up the phone, gave his credit card to the attendant at the service station, said to Della Street, "Come on, Della, we're going to start getting things unscrambled."

They drove down to Santa Monica, then up along the beach where a high, angry surf was pounding on their left. Mason slowed to look for his turnoff, then took a dirt road which branched off and curled upward in a series of twisting curves.

Mason fed gas to the car and handled the wheel with deft skill, keeping well within the limits of safety, yet saving every precious second possible.

102

As Mason's car wound its way up the tortuous road, Della Street said, "What are you going to tell Lauretta Trent if she's there ahead of us, Perry?"

"I don't know," Mason said. "I'll have to remember that *she's* not my client."

"The chauffeur will probably be with her."

Mason nodded.

"And if he should find out that Dr. Alton has now changed his diagnosis and knows that she has been subjected to arsenic poisoning, the man could be dangerous. Lauretta Trent may never get back home."

Mason said, "If I can't talk with her privately I simply might put her in even more danger telling her about the poison. I am not under any obligation to tell Lauretta Trent anything, nor under obligation to withhold anything. I can, of course, ask her to call Dr. Alton and let him break the news to her."

"And then what?"

"Then," Mason said, "George Eagan, the chauffeur, wouldn't necessarily know anything about what has been said. But if she cares enough for him to make him a beneficiary under the will, it will probably take a lot more than a mere telephone conversation to turn her against him; and if I tell her anything, it will turn her against me."

"But Dr. Alton is also a beneficiary under the will."

"We don't know that."

"He seems to think so," she said.

Mason smiled and said, "Also he thought the first attacks were acute food poisoning. Let's see what we can do to take care of our client first. She's our main responsibility. If Lauretta Trent wants to see her, it's for a reason. Let's find out the reason and take it from there."

The road straightened out on a mesa and, within a short distance, Mason saw the lights of the motel.

"Strange place for a motel," Della Street said.

"It's for people going up to the lake for boating and for

fishermen," Mason said. "There just isn't room for a motel on the main highway. It's ocean on one side and sheer bluff on the other."

Mason stopped his car in the parking place, and they walked down the long line of cabins and came to Unit 14.

He tapped on the door.

Virginia Baxter flung the door open. "My gosh, am I glad to see *you!*" she exclaimed. "Won't you come in?"

"Where's Lauretta Trent?" Mason asked.

"I haven't heard another word from her, not a word."

"But she asked you to come out here?"

"Yes."

"Why?"

"She said she had something to tell me. Something of the greatest importance to me."

"And when did this conversation take place?"

"Well, let's see . . . I left your office and went to a branch post office that wasn't too far from my apartment. I sent the letter to myself, registered mail. I had a malted milk, went to my apartment and hadn't been there more than . . . oh, an hour or an hour and a half, when the phone rang and Lauretta Trent told me who she was and asked me if I would meet her."

"Up here at this motel?"

"That's right."

"She gave you directions how to get here or did you know the place?"

"No, she told me exactly how to drive to get here and wanted me to assure her that I'd be leaving right away and wouldn't tell a soul."

"What time did she say she'd meet you?"

"She didn't give me a fixed time, but said she'd be here within an hour after I arrived."

Mason said, "You met Lauretta Trent when she was in the law office where you worked?"

"Yes."

"You were a witness to one of her wills?"

"I think there were two wills, Mr. Mason, and I can't specifically remember being a witness, but I remember drawing up the wills—that is, doing the typing—and I remember there was some peculiar provision in the wills, something about her relatives—there was something unusual about it. She didn't trust her relatives, I know that—that is, she felt they were just waiting for her to die and that their interest in her was purely selfish. I've been trying my best to think what it was that was in at least one of the wills, but somehow I just can't seem to get it clear in my mind. I have that vague recollection— You must remember that we drew lots of wills in the office."

Mason said, "Right at the moment I am not primarily concerned with whether you remember the wills but trying to find out if you remember Lauretta Trent's voice."

"Her voice? No, I wouldn't remember that. I have only a vague recollection of what she looks like, rather a tall, slender woman with hair that was turning gray ... not a bad figure ... you know what I mean, not heavy but ... well-groomed."

"All right," Mason said, "you don't remember anything about her voice?"

"No."

"Then how do you know that you were talking with Lauretta Trent on the telephone?"

"Why, because she told me that— Oh ... oh, I see."

"In other words," Mason said, "a feminine voice on the telephone told you you were listening to Lauretta Trent; that you were to come up here; that Lauretta Trent would meet you here within an hour of the time of your arrival— Now, how long have you been here?"

"Two hours—two hours and a half."

"You registered under your own name?"

"Yes, of course."

"And got this room?"

"Yes."

"And you parked your car?"

"Yes, out in the parking lot."

"Let's go take a look," Mason said.

"But why?"

"Because," Mason told her, "we're checking on everything. I don't like this. You should have followed my instructions and reported to me before you left your apartment."

"But she insisted I was not to tell anyone and that I was to get five hundred dollars and all my expenses if I followed her instructions—and, as I told you, that five hundred dollars looks particularly big to me right now."

Mason said, "She could have promised you a million just as well. If you don't get it, it doesn't make any difference how big it sounded."

Virginia led the way out into the parking lot. "It's right over— Why, that's strange. I thought I left it in that other painted oblong. I'm almost certain I did."

Mason walked over to the car. "You have a flashlight in this car?" he asked.

"No, I don't."

Mason said, "I have one in my car. I'll get it. You don't think this was the place you left the car?"

"Mr. Mason, I'm certain it was not. I remember putting the bumper right up against that stone post over there— That means I was in the parking space to the right."

"Don't touch anything," Mason said. "Stay there. I'll take a look— You've been framed once and got out of it. Perhaps we won't be so fortunate this time."

The lawyer crossed over to his car, took a flashlight from the glove compartment, returned to Virginia Baxter's car and carefully looked over the inside.

"Got your key?" he asked.

Virginia Baxter produced the key. Mason opened the

106

trunk, looked inside, said, "Everything seems to be in order."

He started to walk around the car, then suddenly stopped. "Hello, what's this?" he said.

"Good heavens!" she gasped, "that fender's all dented, and— Look at the front of the bumper, and there's a piece broken—"

Mason said, "Get in the car, Virginia. Start the motor."

Obediently, she jumped into the car, turned on the ignition, started the motor.

Mason said, "Go out of the exit, turn around and come in the entrance to the parking place."

Virginia Baxter switched on the headlights and said, "Only one of the headlights works."

"That's all right," Mason said, "go ahead, go out the exit, turn around and come back in through the entrance."

Mason took Della Street's arm, hurried her over to his automobile.

"You'd better get in, Della, we want this to look as plausible as possible— Get down low in the seat and brace yourself."

Virginia drove her car out of the exit, swung around in a wide loop and turned into the entrance.

Mason's car, running without headlights, made for the entrance, then swung in a swift turn just as Virginia Baxter entered.

Her headlight picked up his car. She slammed on the brakes. Tires screamed a protest. Then there was a crash and the sound of breaking glass as Mason's car hit hers.

Doors opened in the various motel units. The office door opened, and the manager came running out to stand looking at the scene of the accident. Then she came striding toward them.

"Good heavens, what happened?"

Virginia Baxter said, "You— Why, you didn't have your lights on— You didn't tell me—"

Mason said, "I goofed. I should have gone out the exit."

The manager whirled to face Perry Mason. "This is your fault," she said. "Can't you see that sign there? That says ENTRANCE just as plain as day. This is the fourth accident we've had here and that's why I had those big signs put up and knocked a section of the wall down so that the EXIT would be at the other end of the parking lot."

"I'm sorry," Mason said. "It was my fault."

The manager turned to Virginia Baxter. "Are you hurt?"

"No," she said. "Fortunately, I was going slow and I put on my brakes."

The manager turned back to Mason. "Have you been drinking?" she asked.

Mason turned half away from her. "No," he said.

"Well, I think you have—that sign there is just as plain as day— Now, let me see, dearie, you're registered here in the motel, aren't you? Unit Fourteen?"

"That's right."

"Well," she said, "if you want me as a witness you just call me any time. I'm going to call the highway patrol."

"That won't be necessary," Mason said. "It was my fault. I accept the responsibility."

"I'll say it was your fault. You've been drinking. You aren't staying here, are you?"

"I would like to see about getting a room."

"Well, we don't have any rooms left. And we don't cater to drinking parties. You wait right here and don't try to move those cars. I'm calling the police."

The manager turned and marched back to the office.

"What in the world," Virginia Baxter asked, getting Mason to one side, "were *you* trying to do?"

"Insurance," Mason told her.

"Insurance?" she exclaimed.

"Exactly," Mason said. "Now if anyone asks you how your car got smashed up, you can tell them. Moreover, you have witnesses to prove it. You'd better go to your friend, the manager, and see if you can borrow a broom and we'll sweep this broken glass out of here; borrow a dustpan and dump it all in a trash barrel somewhere. You have one headlight and I have one headlight. It looks very much as though we're going to spend the night here unless I get busy and have a rental car delivered to me here. In which event, I'll give you a ride home."

"And our cars?" she asked.

Mason smiled and said, "After the police come, we'll try and get yours back to the parking lot. As far as mine is concerned, I think I'll have the garage tow it away."

Chapter 16

Harry Auburn, the traffic officer who was summoned by the manager, was very polite, very efficient and very impersonal.

"How did this happen?"

"I was coming out," Mason said, "and this young woman was coming in."

The manager said belligerently, "He flagrantly violated the traffic rules of this parking place. There's a sign over there that says EXIT in letters two feet high."

Mason said nothing.

The traffic officer looked at him.

Mason said, "I will report the facts. I was driving out of the parking place. I was coming out to the road through this opening. The young lady was coming in."

"Didn't you see this sign ENTRANCE ONLY?" the traffic officer asked.

Mason said, "My insurance company has instructed me that, in the event of any accident, I am not to say anything that would admit liability in any way. Therefore, I will have to advise you that I am adequately insured and that the facts speak for themselves."

"He's been drinking," the manager said.

The officer looked inquiringly at Mason.

"I had a cocktail before dinner some two hours ago," Mason said. "I have not had anything since."

The officer went to his car, produced a rubber balloon. "Mind blowing this up?" he asked Mason.

"Certainly not," Mason said.

He blew up the rubber balloon.

The traffic officer took it over to a testing machine and, after a few minutes, returned and said, "You don't have enough alcohol to register."

"He's drunk," the manager said.

Mason smiled at her.

"Or he may be drugged," she said.

Mason handed the officer one of his cards. "You can always locate me," he said.

"I recognized you," the officer said, "and, of course, checked your name on your driving license."

"I think that's all that needs to be done here," Mason said. "I will need a tow car."

"I'll phone for one," the officer said, then moved over to his automobile, climbed into the seat, picked up the microphone of his radio and called a number.

After a while, a voice came over the radio speaker. The officer turned down the volume, raised the windows on his car so that the voice was inaudible outside of the car. He talked for some two or three minutes, then he hung up the phone and came back to Virginia Baxter.

"Where have you been this evening, Miss Baxter?" he asked.

"I drove from my apartment to the motel here."

"Make any stops along the way?"

"No."

"Where is your apartment?"

"The same address that's on my driver's license—422 Eureka Arms Apartments."

"Have any trouble along the way?" the officer asked.

"Why, no. Why do you ask?"

The officer said, "There's been a pretty bad accident down on the coast road. George Eagan, a chauffeur, was driving Mrs. Lauretta Trent, going south, when a car veered out of control, crowded the Trent car off the road, struck the rear fender, sent the car into a spin and into the ocean.

111

Eagan escaped, but the car went over the road into the ocean. Lauretta Trent was drowned. They haven't as yet recovered her body.

"The description of the car that caused the accident matches the description of this car— You're sure *you* haven't been drinking?"

"Give her a test," Mason said.

"You have any objection to taking a test?" the officer asked.

She looked at Mason with wide, frightened eyes.

"Not in the least," Mason said.

The officer didn't even turn but kept his eyes on Virginia Baxter.

"No," she said, "I'll take a test."

"Blow up this balloon," the officer said.

Virginia Baxter blew up the balloon. The officer again retired to his automobile, again talked for a while into the microphone, then returned.

"You been taking any drugs today, Miss Baxter?"

"Not today. I took a couple of aspirin last night."

"And that's all?"

"That's all."

"What time did you leave your apartment?"

"Well, let's see, it was about . . . well, probably three hours ago."

"And you came directly here?"

"Yes."

"How long have you been here?"

"You can check the time of registration," Mason suggested.

The manager said, "We don't keep a time record—only the date—but I think she's been here for . . . well, say an hour and a half anyway."

"But I've been here longer than that," Virginia said.

"Well, I'm willing to swear to an hour and a half," the manager said.

The officer looked thoughtful.

"May I ask how they got a description of the Baxter car?" Mason asked.

The officer regarded him thoughtfully, then said, "A motorist, coming along behind, saw the accident. The car turned off on the road that came up here. He got a description of the rear of the car, and a part of the license number."

"Which part?" Mason asked.

"Enough to make a pretty good identification," the officer said shortly.

Virginia Baxter suddenly burst out angrily. "All right," she said, "I've taken all I'm going to take. This is just another frame-up!

"I didn't have any accident along the road; I didn't run into Lauretta Trent's car, and as far as that chauffeur is concerned, he's a plain liar.

"He's been after me to make a forged will for Lauretta Trent and—"

"Easy, easy," Mason interrupted.

"I'm *not* going to take it easy," she stormed. "This chauffeur paid me to make a forged will. He's been planning murder and—"

"Shut up!" Mason snapped.

Virginia turned indignant eyes on him. "I don't have to keep quiet and—"

"You let me do the talking for a minute, Virginia."

The officer said, "You representing this woman?"

"I am now," Mason said.

The traffic officer went over to his automobile, picked up the microphone. This time, he left the door open so they could hear what he said.

"Auburn, at Car two-fifteen. I'm reporting from the scene of the accident at this motel.

"You can't tell a thing about the condition of this car Virginia Baxter was driving because Perry Mason slammed

113

into it with his automobile. Apparently, Perry Mason is representing her as her attorney, and she says George Eagan, the Trent chauffeur, paid her to make a forged will and has been planning a murder.

"That's her story."

The voice that came over the intercommunicating system was loud enough for everyone to hear. It was a crisp voice, filled with authority. It said, "This is the chief investigator of the D.A.'s office. Bring that girl in for questioning. She'll probably be charged with first-degree murder. But let's get the story before Mason mixes up any more of the evidence."

"Very well, sir," the officer said.

"Start now," the crisp voice commanded, "and I mean now!"

"Shall I give her a chance to get her things and—"

The voice interrupted. "Now."

Mason said in an undertone, "This is just what I was afraid of, Virginia. You're mixed up in some sort of a plot. Now, for heaven's sake, keep quiet. Don't tell them *anything* unless I am present."

"That's going to make it look all the worse," she whispered. "They'll find that registered letter I sent myself and—"

The officer interrupted, "Right in this car, Miss Baxter, please."

"I'm certainly entitled to get my things," she said. "I—"

"Under the circumstances," the officer interrupted, "you're under arrest. If I have to, I can put handcuffs on you."

"What's going to happen with this driveway blocked?" the manager asked. She had been standing as an open-mouthed spectator but had finally gotten her breath restored.

"We'll send a wrecking car," the officer said. "In the meantime, I have other things to do."

114

He slammed the door of the car, started the motor, skidded out of the exit, hit the highway, turned on his red light, and the manager, Della and Mason listened to the scream of his siren vanishing in the distance.

Mason surveyed the wreckage ruefuly. "Well," he told Della, "we are, for the moment, immobilized. The first thing to do is to arrange for transportation."

Chapter 17

It was ten o'clock in the morning. Mason paced the attorney's room at the jail impatiently.

A policewoman brought Virginia Baxter in, then discreetly withdrew out of earshot.

Mason said, "I understand you told the police everything, Virginia."

She said, "They kept after me until way late—it must have been nearly midnight."

"I know," Mason said sympathetically. "They told you that they wanted to clear you so you could go home and go to bed; that if you'd only tell them the truth they'd investigate it and, if it checked out, they'd release you immediately; that, of course, if you refused to say anything that was your privilege but, in their own minds, it would show them that you were guilty and they'd stop trying to clear you. In that event they'd go home and go to bed and leave you in jail."

Her eyes widened with surprise. "How did you know what they said?" she asked.

Mason merely smiled. "What did you tell them, Virginia?"

"I told them everything."

Mason said, "Hamilton Burger, the district attorney, and Lieutenant Tragg told me they wanted me here this morning; that they were going to ask you some questions that they thought I should hear. Now, that means something pretty devastating. They evidently have some unpleasant surprises for you.

"It also means that you finally told them you wanted to get in touch with me and they then complied with the law by putting through a call to my office."

"That's exactly what happened," she said. "I told them everything last night because they said they'd investigate and, if I was telling the truth, I could go home and go to bed.

"Right after I'd told them everything, they simply got up and said, 'Well, Virginia, we'll investigate,' and started to walk out.

"I told them that they said I could go home and go to bed, and they said, Why, of course I could, but not tonight. It would be the next night—that it would take a day to investigate."

"Then what?"

"I didn't sleep hardly a wink—being behind bars for the second time— Mr. Mason, what *is* the matter?"

"I don't know," Mason told her, "but a great deal depends on whether you've told me the truth or whether you're lying."

"Why should I lie to you?"

"I don't know," Mason said, "but you've certainly been mixed up in some bizarre adventures, if one believes your story."

"And suppose one doesn't believe it?"

"Well," Mason said, "I'm afraid the district attorney and Lieutenant Tragg of the Homicide Squad are two people who don't believe you."

"Would you expect them to?"

"Sometimes they believe people," Mason said. "They're actually trying to do a job. They're trying to do justice but of course they don't like to have unsolved homicides."

"What about the homicide?" she asked.

Mason said, "George Eagan, the chauffeur, was driving Lauretta Trent down the coast highway. They were coming south from Ventura.

"Mrs. Trent told the chauffeur that she'd tell him where to turn off, that they were going to a motel up in the mountains.

"They approached the turnoff leading up to the motel where you were waiting. So far the facts seem to indicate that Lauretta Trent was the one who telephoned you and asked you to wait for her there."

"She did, Mr. Mason. She did. I told you—"

"You don't know," Mason interrupted. "All you know is that a feminine voice told you that it was Lauretta Trent speaking and you were to go up there and wait at the motel.

"Anyway, just as the chauffeur was preparing to make the left turn, a car came up behind him fast. He swung to the right of the road so as to let the second car get by. However, that car swung over and crowded the Trent car right off the road and over the edge.

"There was an angry surf, and the chauffeur, George Eagan, knew there was deep water down there. He yelled to Mrs. Trent to jump and he flung the car door open and jumped himself. He apparently hit his head on a rock. In any event he was unconscious for some period of time.

"When he came to, there was no sign of the Trent automobile. The highway patrol was there. The highway police got a tow car, sent down divers and located the Trent car. They got grappling hooks on it, used a winch, brought it to the surface. There was no sign of Mrs. Trent, but the door on the left-hand, rear side of the car was unlocked and open. Evidently she had opened that door before the car went over the grade and rolled into the surf.

"They may never recover her body. There are treacherous currents there and a terrific undertow. Skin divers who went down there looking around had a hard time wrestling with the currents. A body could have been carried out to sea or swept down the coast. There's a terrific riptide at that point."

"But why pick on me?"

"The chauffeur got a quick look at the rear end of the car that hit him. The description matches your car. A man who was two cars behind got a look at the last two figures on the license plate and they're the same as yours."

"But I didn't leave the motel," she said.

Mason said, "They picked up some glass at the place where the car had been crowded over the road. There were fragments of a glass headlight. Then the police went up to the motel where I ran into you with my car and examined the glass up there. They found a piece that had broken out of your headlight. The broken piece fits exactly into the lens on your headlight. Then the broken piece of glass that they found down where Lauretta Trent was crowded off the road also fits into the piece of glass that came out of that same headlight. By putting the whole thing together, they have patched up the glass fragments like a jigsaw puzzle and have virtually everything. There is only one small, triangular piece of glass that is missing."

"But that chauffeur," Virginia Baxter said, "why should they believe him when he did all those things?"

"That," Mason said, "is something I don't understand myself. You told them about the chauffeur?"

"Of course."

"About his wanting to bribe you to forge a copy of the will?"

"Yes."

"And about the way you made the carbon copies and mailed them to yourself?"

"Yes. I told them everything, Mr. Mason. I realize now that I shouldn't have, but once I started talking—well, I was just . . . I was just scared stiff. I wanted so desperately to convince them and have them turn me loose."

Abruptly, the door opened. District Attorney Hamilton Burger, accompanied by Lieutenant Tragg, entered the room.

"Good morning, Virginia," Hamilton Burger said.

He turned to Perry Mason. "Hi, Perry. How's everything this morning?"

"How are you, Hamilton?" Mason said. "You going to turn my client loose?"

"I'm afraid not," Burger said.

"Why not?"

"She told us quite a story about George Eagan, the chauffeur for Lauretta Trent," Hamilton Burger said. "It was a nice story, but we don't believe it.

"Lauretta Trent's relatives told us quite a story about the chauffeur. It's a plausible story but it doesn't check out in some details. We're beginning to think that your client *may* be tied in with Lauretta Trent's relatives, trying to discredit Eagan and obscure the issues; incidentally, covering up attempts they have made at committing murder—a murder which was actually consummated by your client."

"Why, that's absurd," Virginia exclaimed. "I never met Lauretta Trent's relatives in my life."

"Perhaps," Mason said, "if you wouldn't be so hypnotized by an act put on by that chauffeur, you might have a clearer understanding of the situation."

"Well, we'll see about that," Burger said.

He stepped to the door, opened it and said to someone outside, "Come in."

The man who entered was in his forties. He had a shock of coal-black hair, dark complexion, high cheekbones, and intense black eyes.

He shifted his eyes from Hamilton Burger to look directly at Virginia Baxter, then shook his head emphatically.

"Have you ever seen this young woman before?" Burger asked the man.

"No," he said shortly.

"There you are," Burger said, turning to Virginia.

"Well, *that's* nothing," she said. "I've never seen him before either. He looks in a general way like the Trent chauffeur, but he's not the man who called on me."

120

"This," Lieutenant Tragg announced dryly, "is George Eagan, the chauffeur for Lauretta Trent. . . . That's all, George, you may go now."

He turned to Mason and said, "George hit his head when he tumbled out of that automobile. He was unconscious for an undetermined length of time."

"Now, just a minute," Mason said. "Just a minute. Don't pull that stuff with me. If he's able to be out walking around and come here to identify, or fail to identify, my client, he can answer a question."

"He doesn't have to," Hamilton Burger said.

Mason ignored the district attorney's comment, said to the chauffeur, "You have a private automobile. It's an Olds and the license number is ODT062."

Eagan looked at Mason with surprise. "That's my license number," he said, "but it isn't an Olds, it's a Cadillac."

"You were driving your automobile day before yesterday?" Mason asked.

Eagan looked at him with a puzzled expression on his face, then slowly shook his head. "I was chauffeuring Mrs. Trent. We drove up to Fresno."

Burger said, "That's all, George. You don't need to answer any more questions."

The chauffeur walked out.

Hamilton Burger turned to Mason and gave an expressive shrug of the shoulders. "There you are," he said. "If any attempt has been made to frame anyone, it's an attempt to frame this chauffeur. You'd better check the story of your client a little bit yourself.

"We'll arraign her at eleven o'clock this morning if that meets with your convenience, and we'll have her preliminary hearing at any time you suggest. We want to give you ample opportunity to prepare."

"That's very nice of you," Mason said, "under the circumstances. We'll have a preliminary just as soon as the

121

judge can get it on the calendar—tomorrow morning, if possible."

Burger's smile was frosty. "You may catch us unprepared on *some* points, Perry, but you won't catch us with our wearing apparel disarranged. This is one case where you're on the wrong end. Your client is a shrewd, scheming opportunist.

"I don't know yet who she's teamed up with. I don't know who administered the poison to Lauretta Trent, but I do know that it was your client's car that crowded her off the road, and your client has told enough lies to make her exceedingly vulnerable.

"At least we'll get her bound over while we're looking for the other conspirator.

"And now, we'll leave you alone with your client."

Burger nodded to Lieutenant Tragg, and the pair walked out, closing the door behind them.

Mason turned to Virginia Baxter.

She said, "There's been a horrible mistake somewhere, Mr. Mason. That man has the general physical characteristics of the chauffeur— I mean, the man I talked with, the one who gave me the name of Menard. . . . Of course, *you* were the one who told me he was Lauretta Trent's chauffeur."

"That," Mason said, "was on the strength of the physical description plus the license number of the automobile he was driving. You're sure it was an Oldsmobile?"

"Yes. It wasn't a new Olds but I certainly thought that's what it was. . . . Of course, I could have made a mistake in the license number; that is, I could have been wrong on the last or something like that, but the first figure was a zero."

Mason shook his head, "No, Virginia, that would be *too* much of a coincidence. But you could have been victimized by someone who inveigled you into doing his dirty work for him. Suppose you try telling me the truth for a change."

"But I have told you the truth."

"*I'll* tell *you* something," Mason said. "If you insist on telling that story, you're going to be bound over for trial on a charge of murder; and if someone is using you as a cat's-paw and you don't give me an opportunity to get you into the clear by telling me exactly what happened, you're in very, very serious trouble."

She shook her head.

"Well?" Mason asked.

She hesitated a moment.

"I've told you the truth," she said at length.

Mason said, "If it's the truth, someone with a diabolically clever mind has carefully inveigled you into a trap."

"It's ... it's the truth," she said.

Mason said, "I'm your attorney. If you insist that a story is the truth, no matter how weird or bizarre it sounds, I have to believe you and not show the slightest doubt when we get to court."

"But you don't really believe me?" she asked.

Mason regarded her thoughtfully. "If you were on a jury and a defendant told a story like that, would you believe her?"

Virginia Baxter started to cry.

"Would you?" Mason asked.

"No," she sobbed, "it sounds too ... too—just too much of a series of improbable things."

"Exactly," Mason said. "Now then, you have one defense and only one defense. Either tell me the absolute truth and let me take it from there, or stay with this improbable story. If you do that, I'm going to have to adopt the position that some shrewd, diabolically clever individual is deliberately framing you for murder. And the way events have been taking place, he's very apt indeed to have you convicted."

She looked at him with tearstained eyes.

"Of course, you realize my predicament," Mason said. "Once I adopt the position that you're being framed, if even the slightest part of your story turns out to be false, you'll be swept along into the penitentiary on a tide of adverse public opinion. The slightest falsehood will completely ruin your chances."

She nodded. "I can see that."

"Now then," Mason said, "in view of that situation and in view of that statement, do you want to change your story?"

"I can't change it," she said.

"You mean because you're stuck with it?" Mason asked.

"I just can't change it, Mr. Mason, because it's the truth. That's all."

"All right," Mason told her. "I'll take it from there and do the best I can with it. Sit tight."

The lawyer walked out.

Chapter 18

Jerry Caswell, the deputy district attorney who had prosecuted Virginia on the charge of possessing narcotics and apparently firmly believed that there had been a miscarriage
of justice in that case, had requested the district attorney's
office to be permitted to present the People's case against
Virginia Baxter at the preliminary hearing.

Now he entered upon his duties with a personalized zest
and a grim determination that Perry Mason was not going
to get any advantage because of ingenuity or quick thinking.

As his first witness, he called George Eagan.

The chauffeur took the stand, testified as to his name, address and occupation.

"Could you tell us what you were doing on Wednesday
night?" Caswell asked.

"I was driving Lauretta Trent in her automobile. We had
been to Ventura and were returning along the coast highway."

"Did you have any fixed destination in mind?"

"Mrs. Trent told me that she intended to turn off to go
up to a motel that was up in the hills near a lake. She said
she would tell me what road to take."

"She didn't tell you what road she intended to take?"

"No, just that she would tell me when to make the turn."

"Now then, are you familiar with the motel known as the
Saint's Rest and the road leading to it?"

"Yes, sir. The turnoff is approximately three hundred
yards to the north of the Sea Crest Café."

"When you approached that turnoff on Wednesday night, what happened?"

"Mrs. Trent asked me to slow down slightly."

"And then what?"

"Well, I realized, of course, that she was going to—"

"Never mind what you thought," Caswell interrupted. "Just confine yourself to answering questions as to facts. What happened?"

"Well, there were headlights coming behind and, since I— Well, I don't know how to express it without saying what I was thinking, but I was preparing for a left turn so I turned—"

"Never mind what you were preparing for; state what you *did*."

"Well, I swung far over to the right-hand side of the road, just as far as I could get, and waited for this car to pass."

"And did the car pass you?"

"Not in the normal manner."

"What did happen?"

"The car suddenly swerved, its front end hit the front end of my car, then the driver jerked the steering wheel so that the hind end swung over and crashed hard against the front end of my car. It knocked my front end way over, and the car went out of control."

"And what happened?"

"I fought the steering wheel, trying to keep the car from going over the bank, but I felt the car going. I shouted to Lauretta Trent to open the door and jump, and I opened my door and jumped."

"Then what happened?"

"I don't know what happened immediately after that."

"You were unconscious?"

"Yes."

"Do you know when you regained consciousness?"

"No. I had no way of knowing the exact time. I know

126

about the time of the accident but I didn't look at my watch to determine the time until sometime later. I was upset and excited and I was feeling bad. I had a terrific headache and I was . . . well, I was groggy."

"How long do you think you were unconscious?"

"Objected to as incompetent, irrelevant and immaterial and no proper foundation laid, calling for a conclusion of the witness," Mason said.

"The objection is sustained," Judge Grayson ruled.

"Oh, if the Court please," Caswell said, "there are certain ways by which a person can tell how long he has been out—certain bits of circumstantial evidence."

"Let him give the circumstantial evidence then and not the conclusions he has drawn from that evidence."

"Very well," Caswell said. "Now, when you regained consciousness, what was your position?"

"I was sprawled out on the ground, face down."

"How near the road were you?"

"I don't know the exact distance, probably about ten feet, I would estimate."

"Who was there?"

"An officer of the highway patrol was bending over me."

"Did he assist you to your feet?"

"Not right away. He turned me over. They gave me some sort of a stimulant, then they asked me if I could move any toes. I could. Then they asked me if I could move my fingers. I could. Then they had me move my legs slowly, then my arms. Then they helped me to a sitting position, then to my feet."

"Do you know where they had started from?"

"Only from what they told me."

"How long was it after you regained consciousness before you were helped to your feet?"

"A couple of minutes."

"And then you looked for the Trent car?"

"Yes."

"Did you see it?"

"No. It was gone."

"And you told the officers what had happened?"

"It took me a little while to collect my senses. I was rambling a little at first."

"Then what happened?"

"Then there was the sound of sirens, and a wrecking car came up, and shortly after that another car came, divers went down into the water and located the Trent car in about twenty-five feet of water. The car was lying on its right side with the front end down; the left-hand doors were open. There was no one in the car."

"How do you know there was no one in the car?"

"I was there when the car was brought to the surface. I ran to it and looked inside. There was no sign of Lauretta Trent."

"Now, if the Court please," Caswell said, "I would like to withdraw this witness temporarily in order to ask questions of another witness. However, I am aware of the fact that when I start to prove admissions made by the defendant, the objection will probably be made that no *corpus delicti* has been established. I wish to state to the court that we are prepared to meet this objection here and now; that the *corpus delicti* means the body of the crime and not the body of the victim.

"There are several instances on record where murderers have been successfully prosecuted, convicted and executed where the body of the victim was never found. It is proper to prove the *corpus delicti* by circumstantial evidence just as any other factor in the case and—"

"You don't need to try to educate the court on the elementals of criminal law," Judge Grayson said. "I think under the circumstances a *prima facie* showing has been made. If Mr. Mason wishes to adopt the position that no *corpus delicti* has been proven, I think he has the laboring oar."

128

Mason got to his feet and smiled. "On the contrary, Your Honor, the defense feels certain that the evidence now introduced is sufficient to prove the death of Lauretta Trent. We intend to make no issue in this case of *corpus delicti* as far as the missing body is concerned. However, the Court will bear in mind that the *corpus delicti* consists not only of proof of death but proof of death by unlawful means.

"So far, it appears that Lauretta Trent's death could well have been an accident."

"That is why I wish to withdraw the witness at this time and put on another witness," Caswell said. "By this witness I can prove that this was a crime."

"Very well," Judge Grayson said. "However, the defendant is entitled to cross-examine the witness on the testimony he has given at this time, if he so desires."

"We will wait with our cross-examination," Mason said.

"Very well. Call your next witness," Judge Grayson said.

"I'll call Lieutenant Tragg to the stand," Caswell said.

Tragg came forward and was sworn.

"Were you at the jail when the defendant was brought in and held for investigation?"

"Yes, sir."

"Did you have any talk with the defendant?"

"I did. Yes, sir."

"And did you advise the defendant of her constitutional rights?"

"Yes."

"And what did she say by way of explanation?"

Tragg said, "She told me that Lauretta Trent had telephoned her and arranged a meeting at the Saint's Rest. That she went up there and claimed she had been there for considerably more than an hour. That she became nervous and telephoned Perry Mason. That Perry Mason went up there to join her at the motel. That after he arrived he suggested that they go out and look at her car."

"And then what?" Caswell asked.

"Then they found that her car had been damaged. That a headlight had been knocked out and a fender bent."

"And did Mr. Mason make any suggestions?" Caswell asked gloatingly.

"She said that Mr. Mason told her to get in her car and drive out of the exit, to then turn around and come right back into the entrance. That when she did this, Mr. Mason jumped in his car and ran into her car, thereby compounding the damage so that it would be impossible—"

"Just a minute," Mason said, "I object to the witness giving conclusions. Let him state the facts."

"I'm asking him what the defendant said," Caswell said. "Did the defendant say why this was done?"

"Yes, she said it was done so that it would be impossible to tell when her car was first damaged."

"What else did she tell you?"

"She said that George Eagan, Lauretta Trent's chauffeur, had approached her about forging a copy of a will."

"What sort of a will?"

"A will purported to have been made by Mrs. Trent."

"And did she say what she did in connection with that?"

"She said that she accepted five hundred dollars; that she forged two wills on the stationery of Delano Bannock, an attorney at law, now deceased, who had done work for Mrs. Trent and by whom she had been employed."

"Did she offer any proof of that statement?"

"She said that she had mailed herself a letter by registered mail containing the sheets of carbon which were used in making the forgeries. She said that following the advice of Perry Mason she had used fresh carbon paper so that it would be possible to read the terms of the forged will by holding the carbon papers to the light."

Judge Grayson said, "Now, just a minute. This is asking for confidential advice given a client by an attorney?"

"It is, Your Honor," Caswell said. "It would be manifestly improper for me to show this conversation except by

130

calling for what the *defendant* had said. In other words, if the defendant should be on the stand and I asked her what her attorney told her, that would be calling for a privileged communication, but with Lieutenant Tragg on the stand, I may ask him what the defendant *said* in regard to her actions and in regard to explanation. If at the time of that conversation the defendant chose to waive the privilege of the confidential communication and state what her attorney has told her, then the witness can repeat that conversation.

"That is a chance an attorney has to take when he advises a client to do things which are for the purpose of confusing the law enforcement officers and, in this instance, for the purpose of compounding a felony.

"We will proceed against Mr. Mason in the proper tribunal and at the proper time, but in the meantime, we have a right to show what the defendant said her attorney told her."

Judge Grayson looked down at Mason. "You have an objection, Mr. Mason?"

"Certainly not," Mason said. "I have no objection to bringing out the facts in this case. At the proper time I will show that persons have deliberately framed a crime on this defendant and—"

"Just a moment, just a moment," Caswell interrupted. "This is not the time for Perry Mason to put on a defense, either for this defendant or for himself. He will have an opportunity to put on a defense for the defendant when I have finished my case and he will have an opportunity to defend himself before the proper tribunal."

"I think that's right," Judge Grayson ruled. "However, Mr. Mason has an opportunity to argue this point in regard to the objection."

"There hasn't been any objection," Mason said. "I want the witness to state what the defendant told him, to state everything the defendant told him."

"Very well, go ahead," Judge Grayson said. "I thought

131

there might be an objection interposed on the ground that this was calling for a privileged communication. However, I can appreciate that once the client has waived the privilege of the communication and made a voluntary statement— Well, there seems to be no objection, go ahead."

"She stated that the witness, George Eagan, had been the one who called on her?"

"Yes."

"And positively identified him?"

"Yes."

"Cross-examine," Caswell snapped.

Mason said, "You were talking with this young woman late at night, Lieutenant?"

"Yes, she was not arrested until rather late in the evening."

"You knew that she was my client?"

"No."

"You didn't?"

"I only knew what she told me."

"And you didn't accept that as true?"

"We never accept what an accused defendant tells us to be the truth. We investigate every phase of the story."

"I see," Mason said. "Then you aren't prepared to state that what she told you about what I had advised her was the truth?"

"Well," Tragg said, hesitating, "there were certain corroborating circumstances."

"Such as what?"

"She gave us permission to pick up the registered letter which was sent to her and to open it."

"And you did that?"

"Yes."

"And found the carbon copies of the purported will just as she had told you?"

"Yes."

"And for that reason you became inclined to believe *everything* she told you?"

"It was a corroborating circumstance."

"Then why didn't you believe her when she said that I was representing her?"

"Well, if it's material," Tragg said, "I did."

"Then why didn't you notify me that she was in jail?"

"I told her she could call you."

"And what did she say?"

"She said there was no use. That she couldn't understand what had happened but that this chauffeur, George Eagan, was the culprit and that she was freely and voluntarily telling us all of these facts so that we could go and pick up Eagan."

"And did you?"

"Not that night. We did the next morning."

"And what happened then?"

"In the presence of Hamilton Burger, the district attorney of the County, and in your presence there at the consulting room of the county jail we confronted the defendant with George Eagan. He said in her presence that he had never seen her before, and she stated that he wasn't the man who had called on her."

"Did she make any further statements?"

"She admitted that the man who called on her had never told her he was George Eagan, the chauffeur, but said that an identification had been made from a physical description and the license number on an automobile. She said that the man who called on her had given the name of George Menard."

"And you got the defendant to tell you all this by telling her that you were investigating the murder; that you wanted to apprehend the guilty person; that you didn't think she could be guilty; that she was too nice a young woman to be guilty of any crime of this sort; that you thought someone was trying to frame her and that if she would give you the facts immediately and without waiting to get in touch with me in the morning, that you would start an investigation which would perhaps have everything all cleared up so that she could go home and spend the night in her own bed. Isn't that right?"

Lieutenant Tragg smiled. "Well, I didn't say that personally, but one of the officers who was present made statements to that effect."

"This was in your presence and with your approval?"

The lieutenant hesitated for a moment, then said with a dry smile, "It is routine in dealing with a certain type of suspect."

"Thank you," Mason said, "that's all."

Caswell said, "Will Carson Herman please take the stand."

Herman proved to be a tall, slender man with a mosquito-beak nose, watery blue eyes, a firm mouth, high cheekbones and an emphatic way of speaking.

He testified that he had been driving south on the coast highway. That is, he was headed between Oxnard and Santa Monica. There were two cars ahead of him. One of them was a light-colored Chevrolet; the car ahead of the Chevrolet was a big, black sedan. He hadn't had an opportunity to make sure of the make of the car. "Did you notice anything unusual?" Caswell asked.

"Yes, sir, as we approached a turnoff road the black car swung far over to the right, apparently wanting—"

"Never mind what you think the driver wanted," Caswell interrupted, "just state what happened."

"Yes, sir. The black car pulled clean over to the shoulder of the road."

"And then what happened?"

"The Chevrolet got almost even with the car; then suddenly swerved over. The front of the Chevy hit the front of the other car a glancing blow and then the driver swung the wheel sharply so that the rear end of the Chevy came crashing against the front of the black sedan."

"Did you see what happened to the black sedan?"

"No, sir. I was following rather close behind the Chevrolet and it all happened so fast that we were past the black car before I had a chance to get a real good look at it. I saw it swerving and tottering and then I was past it."

"Go on. Then what happened?"

"The Chevrolet made a screaming turn up to a side road which takes off up a hill."

"What did you do?"

"I felt that it was a hit-and-run, and as a citizen—"

"Never mind what you felt," Caswell again interrupted, "what did you do?"

"I swung in behind the Chevrolet and tried to follow it so I could get the license number."

"Did you?"

"The road was full of curves, and I tried. I got the last two numerals of the license number, 65. I suddenly realized the road was lonely and realized my predicament. I decided to stop, turn around at the first available opportunity and notify the police.

"Because the road was so lonely and winding, it was certain that the driver of the car ahead would know that I was—"

"Never mind your conclusions," Judge Grayson interrupted. "You have been warned twice, Mr. Herman, we are only interested in facts. What did you do?"

"I slowed to a stop and watched the lights of the car ahead disappear. I may say that as the car swung around so that the headlights shone on the cut bank to the side of the road, I could see that the car had lost one headlight."

"What do you mean it had lost a headlight?" Caswell asked.

"Well, one headlight wasn't working."

"Then what?"

"Then I proceeded very slowly and cautiously until I found a place where I could turn around. I then went back down the road. There was a seafood restaurant about three hundred yards from the turnoff, and I stopped at this restaurant and telephoned the California highway patrol. I reported the accident. They said some motorist had already reported it and they had a radio car on the way."

"You didn't go back to see if the other car had been seriously damaged or any person was injured?"

"No, sir, I'm sorry to say that I didn't. I felt that the first thing to do was to notify the highway patrol. I felt that if any persons were injured, other motorists who had been coming along the highway would see the damaged car, stop and give aid."

"Cross-examine," Caswell said.

"Could you see the car ahead well enough to tell who was driving, whether it was a man or a woman, or how many people were in it?"

"There was only one person in it. I couldn't tell whether it was a man or a woman."

"Thank you," Mason said. "That's all."

Caswell said, "I will now call Gordon Kelvin to the stand."

Kelvin came forward with unhurried dignity, took the oath and testified that he was a brother-in-law of the decedent, Lauretta Trent.

"You have been in the courtroom and heard the testimony of the defendant's statement that she was asked to participate in the forgery of a carbon copy of a will?"

"Yes, sir."

"What can you tell us about the estate of Lauretta Trent?"

"That is objected to as incompetent, irrelevant and immaterial," Mason said.

Caswell retorted quickly, "If the Court please, this is a very material matter. I propose to show that the story told

136

by the defendant was a complete fabrication; that it *had* to be a complete fabrication because the forgery of the carbon copy of a will would have done no good at all. I expect to show by this witness that the decedent, Lauretta Trent, had made a will years before; had given it to this witness in a sealed envelope to be opened at the time of her death; that this envelope was produced and opened and that it contained the last will of Lauretta Trent; that there could be no doubt or ambiguity concerning it and that any so-called carbon copies of other wills would have been completely ineffective."

"I'll overrule the objection," Judge Grayson said.

Kelvin said, "I have always been close to my sister-in-law. I am the elder of the two brothers-in-law.

"My sister-in-law, Lauretta Trent, kept her will in a sealed envelope in a drawer in her desk. She told me where it was some four years ago and asked that it be opened in the event of her death.

"After the tragic occurrence of last Wednesday, and knowing that there might be some question about proper procedure in the matter, I communicated with the district attorney's office and, in the presence of an attorney, a banker, and the district attorney, this envelope was opened."

"What did it contain?"

"It contained a document purporting to be the last will of Lauretta Trent."

"Do you have that document here?"

"I do."

"Produce it, please."

The witness reached in his pocket and produced a folded document.

"You have marked this document in some way so that you can identify it?"

"That document," Kelvin said, "is marked by my initials on each page, by the initials of Hamilton Burger, the district attorney, by the initials of the banker who was present and the lawyer who was also present."

"That should identify it," Judge Grayson said, with a smile. "These, I take it, are your initials written by you, yourself?"

"That's right."

Judge Grayson inspected the document thoughtfully, then handed it to Perry Mason.

Mason studied the document; passed it back to Caswell.

"I want this introduced in evidence," Caswell said. "I suggest that since this is the original will, it may be received in evidence and then the clerk may be instructed to make a certified copy which will be substituted in place of the original will."

"No objection," Mason said.

Caswell said, "I will now read the will into the record, and then it will be filed until a certified copy can be obtained."

Caswell read in a tone of ponderous solemnity: " 'I, Lauretta Trent, being of sound and disposing mind and memory, state that I am a widow; that I have no children; that the only relatives I have in the world are two sisters, Dianne Briggs and Maxine Kelvin; that my sister, Dianne, is married to Boring Briggs and Maxine is married to Gordon Kelvin.

" 'I further state that these four people are living in my house with me and have been for some years; that I am very much attached to my two brothers-in-law, as much so as though they were brothers of mine, and, of course, I have love and affection for my sisters.

" 'I further realize, however, that women—and, in particular, my two sisters—do not have the shrewd, innate business ability which would enable them to handle the numerous problems of my estate.

" 'I, therefore, appoint and nominate Gordon Kelvin the executor of this my last will.

" 'After the specific bequests herein mentioned, I leave

138

all of the rest, residue and remainder of my estate to be divided equally among Dianne and Boring Briggs and Maxine and Gordon Kelvin.' "

Caswell paused impressively as he looked around the quiet courtroom, then turned a page of the will and went on, " 'I give, devise and bequeath to my sister, Dianne Briggs, the sum of fifty thousand dollars; to my sister, Maxine Kelvin, a like sum of fifty thousand dollars.

" 'There have, however,' " Caswell read, and paused to glance around the courtroom significantly, " 'been a few people whose loyalty and devotion have been outstanding.

" 'First and foremost, there has been Dr. Ferris Alton.

" 'Because he has specialized in internal medicine and does not do surgery, he has locked himself in a branch of the profession which is somewhat underpaid as compared with the relatively remunerative practice of medicine in the field of surgery.' "

Virginia Baxter gripped Mason's leg just above the knee with hard fingertips. "Oh, it's so," she whispered. "I remember now. I remember typing that. I remember the tribute she made to—"

"Hush," Mason warned.

Jerry Caswell went on reading. " 'Dr. Alton has given me loyal care and is working himself to death, yet has no adequate reserves for retirement.

" 'I, therefore, give, devise and bequeath to Dr. Ferris Alton the sum of one hundred thousand dollars.

" 'There are two other persons whose loyalty and devotion have made a great impression on me. Those are George Eagan, my chauffeur, and Anna Fritch, who has nursed me whenever I have been sick.

" 'I don't care to have my death an event which will transform these people from rags to riches nor, on the other hand, do I want their loyalty to pass unrewarded.

" 'I, therefore, give, devise and bequeath to my chauffeur, George Eagan, the sum of fifty thousand dollars, in

139

the hope that he will open up a business of his own with a part of this money as capital and save the balance as a reserve. I also give, devise and bequeath a similar sum of fifty thousand dollars to Anna Fritch.' "

Here Caswell turned the page rather hurriedly as one does when nearing the end of an important document.

" 'Should any person, corporation, or otherwise, contest this will or should any person appear claiming that I have a relationship with that person, that he or she is an heir, that I have through inadvertence or otherwise neglected to mention him, I give to such person the sum of one hundred dollars.'

"Now then," Jerry Caswell said, "that will contains the usual closing paragraph with the date. It is signed by the testatrix, and it is witnessed by none other than the late Delano Bannock, the attorney, and . . ." And here Caswell turned impressively to the defendant . . . "the defendant in this case, Virginia Baxter."

Virginia sat gazing at him openmouthed.

Mason squeezed her arm and brought her back to reality.

"Does that conclude the testimony of this witness?" Judge Grayson asked.

"It does, Your Honor."

"Any cross-examination?"

Mason got to his feet. "This will was the one you found in the sealed envelope?"

"Yes. The sealed envelope was in the drawer where Lauretta Trent said it would be. The will was in the sealed envelope."

"What did you do with it?"

"I put it in a safe and called the district attorney."

"Where was the safe?"

"In my bedroom."

"And your bedroom is in the house owned and occupied by Lauretta Trent during her lifetime?"

"Yes."

"The safe was already in your bedroom when you moved in?"

"No, I installed it."

"Why did you install it?"

"Because I had certain valuables and I knew that the house was big; and the reputation of Lauretta Trent for extreme wealth was well known; so I wanted to have a safe place where I could keep my wife's jewelry and such cash as I had in my possession."

"What has been your occupation?" Mason asked.

"I have done several things," Kelvin said with dignity.

"Such as what?"

"I don't think I need to enumerate them."

"Objected to as incompetent, irrelevant, immaterial, not proper cross-examination," Caswell said.

"Oh, certainly," Judge Grayson said, "I think this is background material and cross-examining counsel should be entitled to it, although I can't see that it will affect the outcome of the case or materially affect the evaluation the Court is placing on the testimony of the witness."

"There's no need of going into his entire life," Caswell snapped irritably.

Judge Grayson looked at Mason inquiringly. "Do you have some particular reason for this question?"

"I'll put it this way," Mason said, "so I can summarize the situation. All these various business activities, which you yourself state have been numerous, were unprofitable, were they not?"

"That is not true, no sir."

"But the net result was that you went to live with Lauretta Trent?"

"At her invitation, sir!"

"Exactly," Mason said, "at a time when you were unable to support yourself."

"No, sir. I could have supported myself but I *had* had

141

certain temporary financial losses, certain business set-backs."

"In other words, you were virtually broke?"

"I had had financial troubles."

"And your sister-in-law invited you to come and live with her."

"Yes."

"At your instigation?"

"The other brother-in-law, Mr. Boring Briggs, was living in the house. It was a large house and— Well, my wife and I went there on a visit and we never moved out."

"And the same was true of Boring Briggs, to your knowledge, was it not?" Mason asked.

"What was true?"

"That he had met with financial reverses and had come to live with his wife's sister."

"In his case," Kelvin said, "there were circumstances which made such a course of action . . . well a—necessity."

"Financial circumstances?"

"In a way. Boring Briggs had met with several reverses and was unable to give his wife the monetary advantages which she subsequently obtained through the generosity of her sister, Lauretta Trent."

"Thank you," Mason said. "That's all."

Kelvin left the stand.

"All right," Mason whispered, turning to Virginia Baxter. "Tell me about it."

"That's the will," she answered. "I remember now typing that wonderful tribute to her doctor."

Mason said, "I'm going up to get that will and take a good look at it. I don't want you to seem to be paying any great attention to what I'm doing, but look over my shoulder, particularly at the attestation clause and the witness clause and see if that really is your signature."

Mason walked up to the clerk's desk. "May I see the

142

will, please?" he said. "I'd like to examine it in some detail."

The clerk handed Mason the will while Caswell said, "My next witness will be a member of the California highway patrol, Harry Auburn."

Auburn, in uniform, advanced to the witness stand. He proved to be the officer who had inspected the scene of the collision at the Saint's Rest Motel.

Mason, turning the pages of the will, casually paused to examine the signatures.

Virginia Baxter said in some dismay, "That's my signature and that's Mr. Bannock's signature. Oh, Mr. Mason, I remember it all now. This is the will all right. I remember several things about it. There's a little ink smudge at the bottom of the page. I remember it happened when we were signing it. I wanted to type the last page over but Mr. Bannock said to let it go."

"There seems to be a fingerprint there," Mason said, "a fingerprint in the ink."

"I don't see it."

"Over here," Mason said. "Just a few ridges, but enough, I would say, to make an identifiable fingerprint."

"Heavens," she said, "that will be mine—unless it should be Lauretta Trent's."

"Leave it to Caswell," Mason said, "he'll have found it out."

The lawyer flipped over the remaining pages of the will, folded it, replaced it in the envelope, went up and tossed it casually on the clerk's desk, as though not greatly interested in it, and turned his attention to the witness on the stand.

As Mason walked back and sat down beside Virginia Baxter, she whispered to him, "But why in the world would anyone want all this fuss about forging two wills when there already was this will? It must have been that they didn't know of its existence."

"Perhaps someone wanted to find out," Mason said. "We'll talk it over later, Virginia."

Harry Auburn gave his testimony in a voice without expression, simply relating what had happened, and apparently with every attempt to be impartial but, at the same time, to be one hundred percent accurate.

He testified that he had been directed by radio to go to the Saint's Rest Motel to investigate an automobile accident; that this had been a routine call; that he had gone up the road to the Saint's Rest and found that an automobile belonging to the defendant and one belonging to Perry Mason had been in a collision; that while he was investigating the facts of the collision he asked for a check on the cars, and he was called back on the radio of his car.

"Now, you can't tell us what anyone told you on the radio," Caswell said. "That would be hearsay, but you *can* tell us what you did with reference to that call."

"Well, after receiving that call, I interrogated the defendant as to whether she had been using the car, whether she had been in another collision, and where she had been in the last hour."

"What did she say?"

"She denied using the car except to make that one loop in the motel grounds. She said that she had been in her room in the motel for some two hours. She emphatically denied having been in any other collision."

"Then what happened?"

"I checked the license number of her car; I found two significant figures; I checked the make of the car; I found enough evidence to take her into custody.

"Later on, I returned to the scene of the accident. I picked up pieces of broken headlight which had come from her car; that is, they matched the broken lens on the right-hand headlight.

"I then went to the scene of the accident on the coast road and picked up a bit of glass there which had come

144

from a broken headlight; then I removed the headlight from her car and patched all of the pieces of the glass together."

"Do you have that headlight with you?"

"Yes."

"Will you produce it, please?"

Auburn left the stand, picked up a cardboard carton, opened it and took out an automobile headlight. The lens had been patched together.

"Will you explain these different patchings, please?"

"Yes, sir. These small pieces around the rim were the parts that were in the headlight of the defendant's automobile at the time I found it. I have marked those two pieces number one and number two with pieces of adhesive tape which have been placed on them.

"The pieces of glass I found at the scene of the accident at the Saint's Rest Motel, I numbered number three and number four; and these three pieces, numbers five, six and seven, were picked up at the scene of the hit-and-run on the coast road."

"You may inquire," Caswell said.

"No questions," Mason said cheerfully.

Judge Grayson looked at him. "No questions, Mr. Mason?"

"No questions, Your Honor."

"Now then," Caswell said, "I would like to re-call George Eagan to question him on another phase of the case."

"Very well," Judge Grayson said.

Eagan approached the stand. "You're already under oath," Caswell said.

Eagan nodded and seated himself.

"Did you ever at any time approach the defendant and ask her to tell you about a will?"

"I never saw the defendant in my life until I was taken to see her in the jail."

"You never gave her five hundred dollars or any other sum to make spurious copies of any wills?"

"No, sir."

"In short, you had no dealings with her whatever?"

"That is right."

"Never saw her in your life?"

"No, sir."

"You may cross-examine," Caswell said.

Mason regarded the witness thoughtfully. "Did you," he asked, "know that you were a beneficiary under Lauretta Trent's will?"

The witness hesitated.

"Answer the question," Mason said. "Did you or did you not know?"

"I knew that she had remembered me in her will. I didn't know for how much."

"You knew, then, that when she died you would be comparatively wealthy."

"No, sir. I tell you I didn't know how much."

"How did you know that she had remembered you in her will?"

"She told me."

"When?"

"About three months ago, four months ago—well, maybe five months ago."

"You did a great deal of cooking, preparing foods that Lauretta Trent ate?"

"Yes, sir."

"Outdoor cooking?"

"Yes, sir."

"You used quite a bit of garlic?"

"She liked garlic. Yes."

"Did you know that garlic was a good method of disguising the taste of powdered arsenic?"

"No, sir."

146

"Did you, at any time, put arsenic in the food you prepared?"

"Oh, Your Honor, if the Court please," Caswell interposed. "This is completely incompetent, irrelevant and immaterial. It's insulting the witness and it's calling for matters which have not been mentioned on direct examination. It is improper cross-examination."

"I think it is," Judge Grayson ruled, "unless counsel can connect it up. It is quite all right for him to show that the witness knew he was a beneficiary under the will, but this is an entirely different matter."

Mason said, "I expect to show that a deliberate attempt was made to poison Lauretta Trent by the use of arsenic on three distinct occasions. And on at least one of these occasions, the symptoms followed the ingestion of food prepared by this witness."

Judge Grayson's eyes widened. He sat forward on the bench. "You can prove that?" he asked.

"I can prove it," Mason said, "by pertinent evidence."

Judge Grayson settled back. "The objection is overruled," he snapped. "Answer the question."

Eagan said indignantly, "I never put any poison in Mrs. Trent's food. I don't know anything about any poison; I didn't know she had been poisoned. I knew she had had a couple of spells of severe stomach trouble and I had been told that they would be aggravated by eating highly seasoned foods. I had, therefore, talked her out of having another outdoor feed which she wanted. And for your information, Mr. Mason, I don't know one single, solitary thing about arsenic."

"You knew that you were going to profit from Lauretta Trent's death?" Mason asked.

"Oh, now, just a minute," Caswell said. "This is not a proper interpretation of what the witness said."

"I'm asking him," Mason said, "if he didn't know in his

own mind he was going to profit from Lauretta Trent's death."

"No."

"You didn't know that you would be better off than your monthly salary?"

"Well . . . well, yes. She as good as told me that."

"Then you knew you would profit from her death."

"Not necessarily. I would lose the job."

"But she had assured you that she was going to make it up to you so that there wouldn't be any loss?"

"Yes."

"Then you knew you were going to profit from her death."

"Well, if you want to put it that way, I knew I wouldn't lose anything. Yes."

"Now then," Mason said, "how was Lauretta Trent dressed on this last ride?"

"How was she dressed?"

"Yes."

"Why, she had a hat, coat and shoes."

"What else was she wearing?"

"Well, let's see. She had a topcoat with some kind of a fur, neckpiece rather, that fastened on to the coat in some way."

"And she was wearing that?"

"Yes, I remember she asked me to cut down the car heater because she wanted to keep her coat on."

"She had been where?"

"To Ventura."

"Do you know what she had been doing in Ventura?"

"No."

"Don't you know that she had been looking at some property up there?"

"Well, yes. I know that we drove to a piece of property she had contemplated purchasing and we looked it over."

"And she had a handbag?"

"Yes, of course, she had a handbag."

"Do you know what was in it?"

"No, sir. The ordinary things, I suppose."

"I'm not asking what you suppose. I'm asking what you know."

"How would I know what was in her handbag?"

"I am asking you if you know."

"No."

"You don't know a single thing that was in her handbag?"

"Well, I knew there was a purse in there . . . No, I don't know what was in there."

"As a matter of fact," Mason said, "don't you know of your own knowledge that there was the sum of fifty thousand dollars in cash in that handbag?"

The witness sat bolt upright in surprise. "What?"

"Fifty thousand dollars," Mason repeated.

"Heavens, no! She wasn't carrying any such sum in cash."

"You are positive?"

"Positive."

"Then you know what *wasn't* in her purse."

"I know that she would never have carried any such sum of money with her without telling me."

"How do you know?"

"Just by knowing her."

"Then the only way you know she didn't have that money with her is by reaching a conclusion based upon an assumption. Is that right?"

"Well, when you come right down to it, I don't *know* she didn't have that money with her," the witness admitted.

"I thought so," Mason observed.

"But I'm almost certain she didn't," Eagan blurted.

"Didn't she tell you that she was going to wave a sum of cash under the nose of the owner of this property? Or words to that effect?" Mason asked.

Eagan hesitated.

"Didn't she?" Mason insisted.

"Well," Eagan said, "she told me she was figuring on buying a piece of property up there. And she had told me she felt the owner was up against it for cash and that if she waved the down payment under his nose, he might accept it."

"Exactly," Mason said triumphantly. "And when this automobile was fished out of the water, you were there?"

"Yes."

"And there was no handbag in the bottom of the car?"

"No. I believe the officers failed to find any handbag. The back of the car was completely empty."

"No fur neckpiece? No coat? No handbag?"

"That's right. The officers made an heroic effort to find the body but the divers weren't risking their lives trying to find little objects. As I understand it, the floor of the ocean is rocky there."

"You don't know the driver of the car that hit you?"

"I am told it was the defendant."

Mason smiled. "You yourself don't *know* who the driver of the car was?"

"No."

"You didn't recognize the defendant."

"No."

"It could have been anyone else?"

"Yes."

Mason turned abruptly, walked back to the counsel table and sat down. "No further questions," he said.

Judge Grayson said, "Gentlemen, we got a late start today because of another case which was a carry-over. I am afraid we're going to have to adjourn for the evening."

"My case is just about finished," Caswell said. "I think the Court can receive all of the evidence and make an order disposing of the matter before adjournment. This evidence certainly indicates that a crime has been committed and that

150

there is probable cause to connect the defendant with that crime. That is all that is necessary for us to show in a preliminary examination. I would like to have it completed tonight. I have other matters on my calendar tomorrow morning."

Mason said, "The assistant prosecutor is making a usual mistake in assuming that the case is entirely one-sided. The defendant has the right to put on evidence on her behalf."

"Do you intend to put on a defense?" Judge Grayson asked.

Mason smiled. "Very frankly, Your Honor, I don't know. I want to hear *all* the evidence of the prosecution, and then I want to ask for a recess so I may have an opportunity to confer with my client before making up my mind what to do."

"Under those circumstances," Judge Grayson said, "there is only one course of conduct open to the Court and that is to continue the matter tomorrow morning at ten o'clock.

"Court's adjourned. The defendant is remanded to custody, but the officers are directed to give Mr. Mason a reasonable opportunity to confer with his client before she is taken from the courtroom."

Judge Grayson left the bench.

Mason, Della Street, Paul Drake and Virginia Baxter gathered for a moment in a close huddle at the corner of the courtroom.

"Good heavens," Virginia said, "who was the person who came to me and wanted that forged will made?"

"That," Mason said, "is something we're going to have to find out."

"And how did you know that she had fifty thousand dollars in cash in her purse?"

"I didn't," Mason said, grinning. "I didn't say she had fifty thousand dollars in her purse. I asked Eagan if he didn't know she had fifty thousand dollars in her purse."

"Do you think she did?"

"I haven't the slightest idea," Mason said. "But I wanted to make Eagan say she *didn't* have it.

"Now then, Virginia, I want you to promise me faithfully that you won't talk with anyone about this case before you get into court tomorrow morning. I don't think they'll try to get anything more out of you, but if they do I want you to tell them that you have been instructed not to answer any questions, not to say one single word.

"Do you think you can do that, Virginia, no matter how great the temptation may be to talk?"

"If you tell me to keep quiet," she said, "I will."

"I want you to keep very, very quiet," Mason told her.

"All right. I promise."

Mason patted her shoulder. "Good girl."

He stepped to the door and signaled the policewoman who took Virginia Baxter away.

Mason returned to indicate chairs for the others. He started pacing the floor.

"All right," Paul Drake said, "give. What about the fifty thousand?"

Mason said, "I want a search made for that handbag. I want the officers to make the search. I think they'll do it now.

"Now then, Paul, here's where you go to work. I should have thought of this before."

Drake pulled out his notebook.

Mason said, "Lauretta Trent was intending to have Eagan turn the car to the left and drive up to the Saint's Rest Motel. She had a reason for going there.

"When Virginia told me that Lauretta Trent had telephoned her and told her to go to the Saint's Rest Motel and wait there for her, I felt that perhaps Virginia had been victimized by the old trick of having some third party identify himself or herself over the telephone and, since the telephone doesn't transmit the personal appearance of the per-

152

son talking, it's a very easy matter to deceive someone in a case of that sort.

"However, the fact that Lauretta Trent did intend to turn to the left and go up that road is strongly indicative of the fact that she *had* telephoned Virginia Baxter.

"Now, *why* had she telephoned her?"

Drake shrugged his shoulders, and Mason went on.

"It was either because she wanted to give Virginia some information, on the one hand, or get some information from Virginia, on the other. The strong probabilities are she wanted to get some information from Virginia.

"Now, someone must have overheard that telephone conversation. There's not much chance that the telephone line could have been tapped. Therefore, someone must have heard the conversation at one end of the line or the other. Either someone was listening in Virginia Baxter's apartment, which isn't likely, or someone was listening at the place where Lauretta Trent telephoned."

Drake nodded.

"That person, knowing that Virginia Baxter was going to drive her car to the Saint's Rest, went up to the Saint's Rest, waited until Virginia had parked her car and was inside the motel room. Then that person took Virginia's car, drove it down to the coast highway and waited for Lauretta Trent to come along to keep her appointment.

"That person was a very skillful driver. He hit the Trent car just hard enough to throw it to one side of the road and then speeded up, threw the rear of the Baxter car into a skid which knocked the Trent car completely out of control.

"Then that person drove the crippled Baxter car up to the Saint's Rest Motel and parked it.

"Because other tenants had moved in in the meantime, the parking space where Virginia had parked her car was filled up, so he had to select another parking space."

"Well?" Drake asked.

153

"Then," Mason said, "he presumably picked up his own car, drove it back down to the highway and into oblivion."

Drake nodded. "That, of course, is obvious."

"But is it?" Mason said. "He couldn't tell about the timing element. He couldn't tell whether someone riding along behind got the complete license number of Virginia Baxter's car instead of just the last two numbers. He had to have a second string to his bow."

"I don't get it," Drake said.

Mason said, "He had to have it so he could conceal himself in the event he didn't have time to get back down to the highway. Now, how would he do that?"

"That's simple," Drake said. "He'd rent a unit at the Saint's Rest Motel."

"That," Mason said, "is where you come in. I want you to go to the Saint's Rest Motel, check the registrations, get the license numbers of each automobile and run down the owners. See if you can get a line on anyone who checked in and then left without sleeping in the bed. If so, get a description."

Drake snapped his notebook shut. "All right," he said, "that's a job, but we'll get on it. I'll put a bunch of men on it and—"

"Wait a minute," Mason said. "You're not finished yet."

"No?" Drake asked.

Mason said, "Let's look at what happened after the car was crowded off the road, Paul."

"There were big rocks there," Drake said. "The chauffeur fought for control and lost out. The car toppled over into the ocean—you couldn't have picked a more perfect spot for it. I've checked it carefully. The road makes a left-hand curve there. As soon as you get off the shoulder, there are rocks—some of them eighteen inches in diameter—just regular rough boulders. There's only about ten feet between the road and the sheer drop straight down to the ocean.

"At that point there's an almost perpendicular cliff. The

highway construction crews had to blast a road out of that cliff. It rises two hundred feet above the road on the left and it drops straight into the ocean on the right."

"Presumably," Mason said, "that's why this particular spot was chosen. It would be a perfect place to crowd a car off the road."

"That, of course," Drake said, grinning, "is elemental, my dear Holmes."

"Exactly, my dear Watson," Mason said. "But what happened to Lauretta Trent? The chauffeur told her to jump. Presumably she tried to get out of the car. The door on the left rear was unlatched. There was no body in the car; therefore, she must have been thrown clear."

"Well," Drake asked, "what does that buy us?"

"Her missing handbag," Mason said. "When a woman jumps from an automobile, she hardly bothers to take her handbag with her unless it contains a very, very large amount of money or something that is very, very valuable.

"That was why I had to find out from Eagan whether or not she was carrying something of great value. If she had a large sum of money or something of great value in her handbag, it's quite natural that she'd have told the chauffeur to be alert.

"Yet Eagan's surprise was too natural to be feigned. We're forced to the conclusion that, if there was anything of value in her purse or handbag, he knew nothing about it.

"Yet, when Lauretta Trent was faced with that moment of supreme emergency, that moment of great danger, she either grabbed up her handbag from the seat before trying to jump, or it was washed out of the car—otherwise it would be in the car.

"Now, my questioning about fifty thousand dollars being in the handbag will spur the police to go back and make a desperate search for that handbag with divers and submarine illumination. If the handbag is lying there among the rocks on the floor of the ocean, they'll find it. A body would

155

be carried away by the ocean currents, a handbag would be trapped in the rocks."

Drake gave a low whistle.

"Then, of course," Mason said, "we come to the peculiar conduct of the heirs. Someone was trying to get Virginia to furnish a forged will which could be planted in the office copies of Bannock's wills."

"That is the thing that gets me," Drake said. "With a perfectly good will in their possession, why should anyone want to plant a forged will?"

"That," Mason said, "is what we are going to have to find out—and find out before ten o'clock tomorrow morning."

"And why the *second* spurious will?" Drake asked.

"That," Mason said, "is good practice in will forgeries, Paul. If in some way forged will number two is knocked out, then forged will number one has to be faced.

"Heirs are much more willing to compromise when they have two difficult hurdles to jump."

"Well," Drake said, "it's too much for me. I not only don't think we have the right answer, but I don't think we're even on the right track."

Mason smiled. "What track do you think we're on, Paul?"

"The one that makes Virginia blameless," Drake said.

Mason nodded thoughtfully. "As her attorney, Paul, that's the only track I can see."

Chapter 19

Back in his office, Mason said, "How about working late tonight, Della, and then having dinner?"

Della Street smiled. "You know I never go home until you do when we're working on a case."

Mason patted her shoulder. "Good girl," he said. "I can always depend on you. Put some paper in the typewriter, Della. I'm going to give you a list of questions."

"Questions?" she asked.

Mason nodded. "Somehow I have a feeling that I'm letting my client down in this case simply because I'm not using my head and breaking the case down to basic fundamentals.

"Someone in the background is carrying out a preconceived plan or, rather, has carried out a preconceived plan.

"That plan makes sense to him, but the outward manifestations of it, which we see in the light of events which have taken place, simply don't make sense.

"When that happens, it means we're looking at only a part of the picture. Let's start taking things up one at a time and trying to see if we can get answers.

"We'll start with question number one," Mason said.

"Why did someone plant a shipment of contraband in Virginia Baxter's suitcase?"

Della Street duly typed the question.

Mason started pacing the floor. "First answer," he said, "and the most obvious answer is that this person wanted Virginia Baxter convicted of a felony.

"Question number two: Why did this person want Virginia Baxter convicted of a felony?

"First and most obvious answer is that he knew she was a subscribing witness to Lauretta Trent's will. He intended to do something which would indicate that will was a forgery and, therefore, wanted to be able to weaken her credibility as a witness.

"Question number three: Why did anyone go to Virginia Baxter and ask her to type two fraudulent wills?

"The obvious answer to that, of course, if that he intended to plant those carbon copies somewhere where they could be used to his advantage.

"Next question: Why could those spurious carbon copies be used to his advantage? What did he expect to gain by them?"

Mason, pacing the floor, paused, shook his head and said, "And the answer to that question is not obvious.

"Then we have the question: Why did Lauretta Trent want to talk with Virginia Baxter?

"The obvious answer to that is that she knew, in some way, conspirators were trying to use Virginia Baxter. Probably, she knew about the spurious wills. Or perhaps she just wanted to interrogate Virginia about the location of the carbon copies of the wills Bannock had drawn.

"There again, however," Mason went on, "we run up against a blank wall, because why would Lauretta Trent bother about any will which she was supposed to have executed years ago? If she had wanted to make certain her will was the way she wanted it, she would have gone to an attorney and inside of an hour have had a new will properly executed."

Mason paced the floor for a few minutes, then said, "Those are the questions, Della."

"Well, it seems to me you've got most of the answers," she said.

"The obvious answers," Mason said, "but are they the right answers?"

158

"They certainly seem logical," Della Street said encouragingly.

"We'll put one more question," Mason said. "Why in that moment of supreme danger did Lauretta Trent grab her handbag? Or, putting it another way, why wasn't Lauretta Trent's handbag found in the automobile when the car was fished out of the ocean?"

"Perhaps she had the strap of her handbag over her arm," Della Street said.

"She wouldn't have been riding with the strap over her arm," Mason said. "Even if she'd picked it up at the time of the collision, when she was catapulted into cold ocean water she would at least have tried to swim. When you try to swim, you're using your arms; and when you're using your arms under water, a handbag strap isn't going to stay over your arm."

"Well," Della Street said, "we have a rather imposing list of questions."

Mason paced the floor for a few minutes, said, "You know, Della, when you're trying to recall a name and can't do it, you sometimes think about something else and then the name pops into your mind. I think I'll try thinking about something else for a while and see what happens with these questions."

"All right," she said, "what else would you like to think about?"

"You," he told her, grinning. "Let's drive out someplace where we can have a cocktail and a nice, quiet dinner.

"How about going to one of the mountain resorts where we can sit in a dining room looking out over the lights of the city and feel far removed from everyone and anything?"

"And I take it," Della Street said, pushing back her secretarial chair and putting a plastic cover on the typewriter, "we take this list of questions and answers with us?"

"We take those with us," Mason said, "but we try not to think about them until after dinner."

Chapter 20

Della Street, seated across the table from Perry Mason, regarded him solicitously.

The lawyer had eaten his broiled steak mechanically, as though hardly knowing what he was putting in his mouth. Now, he was sipping after-dinner black coffee, his eyes fixed on the dancing couples who glided over the floor. His gaze was not following any particular couple but his eyes were focused on the sea of lights visible in the valley below through one of the big windows.

Della Street's hand crept across the table, rested reassuringly on the lawyer's hand. Her fingers tightened.

"You're worried, aren't you?"

His eyes swiftly flashed to hers, blinked as he got her in focus, and his sudden smile was warm. "Just thinking, that's all, Della."

"Worried?" she asked.

"All right, worried."

"About your client, or about yourself?"

"Both."

"You can't let it get you down," she said, her hand still resting on his.

Mason said, "A lawyer isn't like a doctor. A doctor has scores of patients, some of them young and curable, some of them old and suffering from diseases that are incurable. It's the nature of life that individuals move in a stream from birth to death. A doctor can't get so wrapped up in his patients that he suffers for them.

"A lawyer is different. He has relatively fewer clients.

Most of their troubles are curable, if a lawyer only knew exactly what to do. But whether they're curable or not, a lawyer can always better his client somewhere along the line if he can get the right combination."

"How about yourself?" she asked.

Mason grinned and said, "I led with my chin. I knew, of course, that someone had taken Virginia's car and that it had become involved in an accident. I felt that it was a trap and someone had made an attempt to frame her.

"If that had been the case, I was perfectly justified in doing what I did.

"As a matter of fact, I was justified anyway. I didn't know any crime had been committed. I did know that an attempt had been made to frame a crime on Virginia a short time earlier and I was trying to protect— Of course, if I'd known a murder had been committed and the car had been involved, then my actions would have been criminal. After all, it's a question of intent."

The lawyer glanced back to the dance floor, his eyes followed a couple for a moment, then again became focused on the distance.

Abruptly he turned to Della Street and put his hand over hers. "Thanks for your loyalty, Della," he said. "I'm not much on putting those things into words. I guess perhaps I take you too much for granted, like the air I breathe and the water I drink, but that doesn't mean I don't appreciate all you do."

He stroked her fingers.

"Your hands," he said, "are wonderfully reassuring. You have competent hands, feminine hands but, nevertheless, strong hands."

She laughed self-consciously. "Years of typing have strengthened the fingers."

"Years of loyalty have strengthened the meaning."

She gave his hand a quick squeeze; then, aware that they were attracting attention, abruptly withdrew her hand.

161

Mason started to look at the distant sea of light again then, suddenly, his eyes widened.

"An idea?" she asked.

"Good heavens," Mason said. He was silent for several moments, then said, "Thanks for the inspiration, Della."

She raised inquiring eyebrows.

"Did I suggest something?" she asked.

"Yes, what you said about typing."

"It's like piano playing," she said. "It strengthens the hand and fingers."

Mason said, "Our second question: *Why* did they want to frame a crime on Virginia Baxter. The answer I gave you is wrong."

"I don't get it," she said. "It's the most logical answer in the world. It seems that would be the only reason they could possibly have for framing a crime on her; then her subsequent testimony could be impeached if she had been convicted of—"

Mason interrupted with a shake of his head. "They didn't want to convict her," he said. "They wanted to be sure that she would be out of the way."

"What do you mean?"

"They wanted to get into her apartment, get her stationery and her typewriter."

"But they knew she was on a plane and—"

"They probably didn't know it in time," Mason interrupted. "She'd only been to San Francisco and had been away overnight. They had to be absolutely certain that they would have access to the typewriter and Bannock's stationery and be absolutely certain that Virginia wouldn't be home until they had done what they intended to do."

"And what did they intend to do?" Della asked.

Mason, his face flushed with animation as his mind speeded over the situation, said, "Good Lord, Della, I should have seen it all a long time ago. Did you notice anything peculiar about that will?"

162

"You mean the way in which she left the property?"

"No. The way in which the will was drawn," Mason said. "Notice that the residuary clause was on the first page.... How many wills have you typed, Della?"

"Heaven knows," she said, laughing. "With all my experience in a law office, I've typed plenty."

"Exactly," Mason said. "And in every one of them, the will has been drafted so that the specific bequests are mentioned and then, at the close of the will, the testator says 'all of the rest, residue and remainder of my estate, of whatsoever nature and wheresoever situated, I give, devise and bequeath to ...' "

"That's right," she said.

Mason said, "They had a will. The last page of it is authentic. Probably the second page is authentic; the first page is a forgery, typed on Bannock's typewriter and on his stationery, but typed within the last few days.

"There's a substitute page in that will—and it had to be done on the same typewriter that was used at Bannock's office and whoever forged it had to have an opportunity to use that typewriter."

"But who forged it?" Della Street asked.

"On a document of that sort," Mason said, "the person or persons who made the forgery are most apt to be the persons who benefited by the forgery."

"All four of the surviving relatives are beneficiaries," she said.

"And the doctor, the nurse and the chauffeur," Mason supplemented.

The lawyer was thoughtfully silent for a moment, then said, "There was one thing about the first case we had for Virginia Baxter that puzzled me."

"What was that?"

"The officer stating that he couldn't divulge the name of the person who had tipped them off, but that person had been thoroughly dependable in his prior tip-offs."

"I still don't get it," Della Street said.

"Whoever wanted to forge that will must have known a police informer, bribed him to give false information and arranged to plant the dope in Virginia's suitcase."

Mason pushed back his chair, jumped to his feet, looked around for the waiter.

"Come on, Della," he said, "we have work to do."

The waiter not being immediately available, Mason dropped a twenty-dollar bill and a ten-dollar bill on the table and said, "That will cover the check and the tip."

"But that's way too much," Della Street protested, "and I have to keep a record of expenses."

"Don't keep a record of these expenses," Mason said. "Time is worth more than keeping accurate records. Come on, let's go."

Chapter 21

Paul Drake was seated in his cubbyhole of an office, at the end of a long, narrow rabbit-warren runway. Four telephones were on his desk. A paper plate with part of a hamburger sandwich and a soiled, greasy paper napkin had been pushed to one side.

Drake had a paper container filled with coffee in front of him. He was holding a telephone to his ear and, intermittently, sipping coffee as Mason and Della Street entered.

"All right," Drake said into the telephone, "stay with it as best you can. Keep in touch with me."

Drake hung up the telephone, regarded the lawyer and his secretary in dour appraisal, said, "Okay, here you come fairly reeking of filet mignon, baked potatoes, French fried onions, garlic bread and vintage wine. I've gagged down another greasy hamburger sandwich, and already my stomach is beginning to—"

"Forget it," Mason interrupted. "What did you find out about the motel, Paul?"

"Nothing that'll help," Drake said. "A man checked in all right, and his bed wasn't slept in. He's probably our man, but the name and address he gave were phony; the license of the car he wrote down was incorrect—"

"But it *was* an Oldsmobile, wasn't it?" Mason asked.

Drake cocked an eyebrow. "That's right," he said. "The car was listed as an Olds. . . . They don't usually dare put a wrong make on the register when they're putting down the make of the car; but they do juggle the license numbers around, sometimes transposing the figures and—"

"The description?" Mason asked.

"Nothing worthwhile," Drake said. "A rather heavyset man with—"

"Dark eyes and a mustache," Mason said.

Drake raised his eyebrows. "How did *you* get all of this?"

"It checks," Mason said.

"Go on," Drake told him.

Mason said, "Paul, how many contacts do you have? That is, intimate contacts in police circles?"

"Quite a few," Drake said. "I give them tips; they give me tips. Of course, they wouldn't let me get away with anything. They'd bust me and take my license in a minute if I did anything unethical. If that's what you're leading up to, I—"

"No, no," Mason said. "What I want is the name of an informer police rely on in dope cases who answers the description of the man who checked in at the Saint's Rest Motel."

"That might be hard to get," Drake said.

"And again, it might not," Mason said. "Whenever they issue a search warrant on the strength of an informer's testimony, or even on the strength of a tip, they have to disclose the source of their information if they want to use the evidence they've picked up. For that reason, there's quite a turnover in informers.

"After an informer becomes too well known, he can't do any more work because the underworld has him spotted as a stool pigeon.

"Now, my best guess is that the man we want has been an informer, has had his identity disclosed to some defense lawyer who, in turn, has tipped off the dope peddlers, and the stool pigeon finds himself temporarily out of a meal ticket."

"If that's the case," Drake said, "I can probably find out who he is with the description we have."

166

Mason gestured toward the telephones. "Get busy, Paul. We're going down to my office."

"How strong can I go?" Drake asked.

"Go just as strong as you have to to get results," Mason told him. "This is a matter of life and death. I want the information and I want it just as fast as I can get it. Put out a dozen men if you have to; get calls through to everybody you know; tell them it's a matter of law enforcement and offer a reward if you have to."

"Okay," Drake said wearily, pushing the paper coffee container to one side, picking up the telephone with his left hand, opening a drawer in the desk with his right, and taking out a bottle of digestive tablets.

"I'll call you as soon as I get anything or, better yet, come down to the office and report."

Mason nodded. "Come on, Della," he said, "we'll wait it out."

Chapter 22

Mason and Della Street were in the lawyer's private office.

Della had the big electric percolator filled with coffee, waiting for Paul Drake.

Mason paced the floor restlessly, back and forth, his thumbs hooked in his belt, his head thrust slightly forward.

At length he stopped from sheer weariness, dropped into a chair and gestured toward the coffee.

Della filled his cup.

"Why did you make all this to-do about the handbag?" she asked. "Do you have any information I don't?"

Mason shook his head. "You know I don't."

"But I haven't heard anything about fifty thousand dollars in cash."

Mason said, "There's something mighty peculiar about this case, Della. Why wasn't the handbag found in the car?"

"Well," Della Street said, "with a wild surf, a stormy night, a car toppled into the ocean—"

"The handbag," Mason said, "would be on the floor of the car. Or, if it fell out, it wouldn't drift far. I didn't say the handbag had fifty thousand dollars in cash; I asked Eagan if he didn't know it had fifty thousand dollars in cash. I wanted to inspire a host of amateur divers to search for that bag. I—"

Drake's code knock sounded on the door of Mason's office.

Della Street jumped to her feet, but Mason beat her to the door and jerked it open.

Drake, his face showing lines of fatigue, said, "I think I've got your man, Perry."

"Who is it?"

"A character by the name of Hallinan Fisk. He has been a long-time stoolie for the police in one of the suburbs but there was one case where the police had to disclose his name and one case where Fisk had to testify. Now he's a known informer. He thinks his very life is in danger. He's trying to get sufficient money from the police undercover fund to leave the country."

"Any hope of success?" Mason asked.

"Probably some," Drake said, "but the police don't have that kind of money. This is a dog-eat-dog world. It's not generally known, but the police in this outlying town sometimes pay off their informers by letting them cut corners.

"Fisk has been giving the police information on big-time stuff and also on dope. He's been making *his* money out of being a runner for a bookmaker. The police closed their eyes to this in return for tips on dope. Now that his occupation as a stoolie is out in the open, the bookmaker is afraid to have him around even though Fisk told the bookmaker he can virtually guarantee him freedom from arrest.

"The bookmaker is afraid that hijackers are going to lift his cash and that he may get himself bumped off. He's had a couple of anonymous telephone calls telling him to get rid of Fisk, or else; and in that business, that's all that is needed to make Fisk as desirable as a guy with smallpox."

"You get his address?" Mason asked.

"I think I know where he can be found," Drake said.

"Let's go," Mason said.

Della got up from her chair, but Drake motioned her down with his hand, "Nix," he said. "This is no place for ladies."

"Phooey," she said. "I know about the birds, the bees, the flowers and the underworld."

"This is going to be tough," Drake said.

Della Street looked appealingly to Perry Mason.

Mason deliberated a moment, then said, "Okay, come on, Della, but you're on your own. . . . How are you fixed for protection, Paul?"

Drake pulled back his coat to show a gun in a shoulder holster.

"If the going gets tough," he said, "we can flash my credentials and, if it comes to a real showdown, we can use this."

"We're dealing with murder," Mason said.

They carefully switched out the lights in the lawyer's private office, locked the door, and went down to Drake's car.

Drake drove down to skid row, which at this hour was a blaze of nighttime activity.

From time to time he looked dubiously at Della Street.

Drake finally found a parking place near the rooming house which was their destination.

Della, tucked in between the broad shoulders of Perry Mason and Paul Drake, was guided across the street along some thirty feet of sidewalk, then up a flight of stairs to a dimly lit little alcove where a counter held a plaque with the word OFFICE on it, and a bell.

Back of the counter were hooks containing various keys.

"Number five," Drake said. "The key isn't on the hook, so we'll take a look."

"He's not apt to be in, is he?" Della asked. "This is the period of high activity for skid row."

"I think he is," Drake said. "I think he's afraid to leave his room."

They walked down a corridor, dark, smelly and sinister.

Drake located No. 5, pointed toward the underside of the door.

"There's a light," he said.

Mason's knuckles tapped a peremptory message on the panels of the door.

170

For a moment there was no answer, then the voice of a man standing close to the door said, "Who is it?"

"Detective Drake," Drake said.

"I don't know any dicks by the name of Drake."

"I have something for you," Drake said.

"That's what I'm afraid of."

"You want me to stand here in the hall and tell it so everybody can hear it?"

"No, no."

"Well then, let us in."

"Who's the 'us'?"

"I have a girl with me," Drake said, "and a friend."

"Who's the girl?"

Della Street said, "My name is Street."

"Well, go find yourself another alley, sister."

Mason said, "All right, if that's the way you want it, that's the way it'll be. You'll pay the price. You wanted to get lost and the deal I have gives you a chance."

"*You* can do the getting lost," the man's voice said. "I'm not opening the door for any crummy gag like this. If you want me to open up, get someone I know."

Mason motioned to Paul Drake, said, "You and Della wait here in the corridor, Paul. If he comes out, nab him."

"What do I do with him?"

"Hold him, one way or another. Push him back in the room. Put him under citizen's arrest if you have to."

"For what?" Drake asked.

"Hit-and-run," Mason said. "But I don't think he'll be out."

Mason walked down the long, smelly corridor to a telephone booth which smelled of stale cigar smoke.

Mason dialed police headquarters. "Give me Homicide," he said, when he had an answer.

A moment later when a voice said, "Hello, this is Homicide," Mason said, "I have to get Lieutenant Tragg on a matter of the greatest importance. How long would it take

171

to get a message through to him? This is Perry Mason talking."

The voice at the other end of the line said, "Just a minute."

A second and a half later Lieutenant Tragg's dry voice came over the wire. "What's the matter, Perry, you found another body?"

"Thank heavens you're there," Mason said. "I'm really in luck."

"You are, for a fact," Tragg told him. "I just dropped in to see if there were any new developments on a case I am working on. What's the trouble?"

Mason said, "I want you to join me. I've got something big."

"A corpse?"

"No corpse, not yet. There may be one later on."

"Where are you?" Tragg asked.

Mason told him.

"Shucks," Tragg said, "that's only a short distance from headquarters."

"Will you join me?" Mason asked.

Tragg said, "Okay."

"Bring a man with you," Mason told him.

"Okay," Tragg said, "I'll grab a police car and be there within a matter of minutes."

"I'm waiting for you at the office at the head of the stairs," Mason told him. "This is a walk-up rooming house, second floor only—over a bunch of hock shops and honky-tonks."

"I thought I knew the dump," Tragg said. "We'll be there."

Mason stood waiting by the phone booth.

Two men came up the stairs, paused at the office, looked furtively around them, saw Mason standing there, started toward him.

The lawyer moved a step or two forward.

172

The men looked at his height, at his shoulders, looked at each other, then wordlessly turned, walked back to the head of the stairs and went down to the street.

A few moments later, Tragg, accompanied by a uniformed officer, came to the head of the stairs, paused and looked up and down the corridor.

Mason came striding forward.

Tragg paused by the counter, waiting for him, looking at the lawyer with kindly, quizzical eyes.

"All right, Perry," he said, "what is it this time? Here's your cat's-paw. Where's the chestnut you want pulled out of the fire?"

Mason said, "Room five."

"How hot is the chestnut?"

"I don't know," Mason said, "but once we get in and shake him down, I think we'll find the solution of the Lauretta Trent murder case."

"You don't think we have it already?"

"I know you don't have it already," Mason said.

Tragg sighed. "I could have saved myself a trip if I'd only been properly skeptical," he said. "What's more, the office takes a dim view of our running around on the hunches of defense attorneys trying to undermine cases the district attorney is prosecuting in court.

"Played up in the newspapers, it wouldn't make a very nice story, now, would it?"

"Have I ever left you in the middle of a story in the newspapers that didn't look good?" Mason asked.

"Not yet," Tragg said. "I don't want you to start."

"All right," Mason told him, "you've come this far, come on down to room five."

Tragg sighed, said to the officer, "Okay, we'll take a look. That's all we're doing, taking a look."

Mason led the way down to where Paul Drake and Della Street were waiting.

"Well, well," Tragg said, "we seem to have a quorum."

173

Mason banged on the door again.

"Go away," the voice inside said.

Mason said, "Lieutenant Tragg of Homicide and an officer."

"You got a warrant?"

"We don't need a warrant," Mason said. "We—"

"Now, just a minute," Tragg interrupted, "I'll do my own talking. What's this all about?"

Mason said, "This man registered under the name of Carlton Jasper at the Saint's Rest Motel. He's also the stoolie who gave the police the bum steer on the dope in Virginia Baxter's suitcase. He's waiting for police funds to get out of town.

"He's been a professional informer for the dope squad and— You want me to stay here and yell the whole business out in the corridors, Fisk?"

There was a sound of a bolt on the door; then a chair being moved. The door opened to the limit of a safety chain. Obsidian black eyes peered out anxiously, came to rest on the police officer's uniform, then looked at Tragg.

"Let me see your credentials," he demanded.

Tragg slipped a leather container from his pocket, held it where the man could see it.

The man said, "Look up and down the corridor. Anybody there?"

"Not now," Mason said, "but a couple of torpedoes came up a few minutes ago. They started down to your room and then turned back when they saw I was a witness."

Shaking hands fumbled with the chain on the catch on the door.

The door opened.

"Come in, come in," Fisk said.

The little group walked into the room—a bedraggled place with a cheap, sagging bed, a paper-thin carpet in which holes had been worn in front of the cheap, pine dresser, its wavy mirror distorting reflections.

There was one cushioned chair, one cane-bottomed, straight-backed chair.

Fisk said, "What is it? You fellows have got to give me protection."

Mason said, "What was the idea of framing Virginia Baxter on that dope, and why did you go to the Saint's Rest and take her car?"

"Who are you?" Fisk asked.

"I'm her lawyer."

"Well, I don't need your type of mouthpiece."

"I'm not a mouthpiece," Mason told him. "I'm a lawyer. And here, my friend, is a subpoena for you to appear in court tomorrow and testify as a witness in the case of People versus Baxter."

"Say, what kind of a dodge are you pulling on me?" Tragg asked. "Getting me down here just so you could serve a subpoena."

"That's all," Mason told him cheerfully, "unless you want to use your head. If you do, you can cover yourself with glory."

"You can't serve me with any subpoena," Fisk said. "I only opened the door for the law."

"How come your fingerprints are all over Virginia Baxter's car?" Mason asked.

"Phooey, you won't find a fingerprint on the thing."

"And," Mason said, "when the officers went to Virginia Baxter's apartment to search it on the strength of your representation that there was dope hidden there, you managed to fix the door so you could get back in with the person who did the typewriting on Virginia's typewriter."

"Words, words, words," Fisk said. "I get so tired of having people try to frame things on me. Listen, lawyer, I've been worked over by experts. You amateurs don't stand a chance."

"You wore gloves in handling Virginia Baxter's car,"

175

Mason said, "but you didn't have gloves on in the Saint's Rest Motel. Your fingerprints are all over the room."

"So what? Sure, I admit I was at the Saint's Rest Motel."

"And registered under an assumed name."

"Lots of people do that."

"And gave a phony license number."

"I wrote it down according to the best way I could remember it."

Mason, looking at the man, said suddenly, "Good heavens, no wonder! There's a family resemblance. What's your relationship to George Eagan?"

For a moment the black eyes looked at Mason with cold defiance.

"That," Mason said, "is something we *can* check."

Fisk seemed to grow smaller inside of his coat. "All right," he said. "I'm his half-brother. I'm the black sheep of the family."

"And," Mason said, "you switched license numbers with Eagan's automobile and of course Eagan didn't notice—that was just in case anyone tried to identify you through the license number."

"Got any proof?" Fisk asked.

"I don't need it," Mason said. "By the time I put you on the witness stand tomorrow and the newspapers publish your picture and the history of your activities as a stool pigeon and double-crosser, the underworld will take care of you a lot better than I can. Come on, folks, let's go."

Mason turned and started to the door.

For a long moment Fisk stood there, then he grabbed Mason's coat sleeve. "No, no! Now, look, look, we can square this thing."

He turned from Mason to Lieutenant Tragg. "I've given you folks the breaks," he said. "You folks can help me out. Get this mouthpiece off my neck. Get me out of town."

Tragg, studying the man intently, said, "You tell us the

whole story and we'll see what we can do. But we're not buying anything blindfolded."

Fisk said, "Look, I've been in trouble, lots of trouble, lots of times in trouble. George had to get me out of it once when I was in bad trouble."

"Who's George?" Tragg asked.

"George Eagan, Lauretta Trent's chauffeur."

Mason and Tragg exchanged glances, then Tragg turned to Fisk and said, "All right, come on, what happened?"

"Well, I lost out with the police and lost all my connections and I was up against it. That was when this woman came to me who had helped out before."

"What woman?"

"The nurse, Anna Fritch. I'd dated her once or twice and I'd furnished her with dope over a period of years."

"Go on," Tragg said.

"She was teamed up with Kelvin. Kelvin thought he was going to get the bulk of the Trent estate—he and his brother-in-law, and their wives, of course. So he got this nurse to hurry the old gal over the divide.

"They made three passes with arsenic. They didn't dare to kill her with arsenic, but she had a bad pump and the idea was that all the upchucking from a small dose would make the pump give out.

"Then while the old dame was being sick the last time, Kelvin found the will. He damn near dropped dead from the shock.

"So he had to change the will. They tracked down the lawyer's typewriter. The nurse was a good typist. If she had plenty of time she swore she could make a forgery they'd never detect, but she needed the lawyer's typewriter and stationery.

"That meant they wanted not only to get Virginia Baxter discredited so she couldn't spill their apples if she remembered the terms of the real will, but they wanted her in the cooler.

"They also wanted to either get Bannock's carbon copy of the real will or else scramble things so no one could ever get to first base by going to the old files—but they didn't think up this angle until later when I raised the question.

"Anyhow, first thing was to get this Baxter woman in the clink and get her convicted of a dope charge.

"Well, I did what I was supposed to. I bribed a guy to let me out to the plane to get my baggage on the ground; that it was an important shipment. I spotted the broad's bag as soon as it came off the plane; then said I'd lost my tags. They told me I had to identify the contents, so I got the suitcases opened and then said I'd made a mistake and, in the confusion, managed to plant the stuff I was to put in the suitcase.

"I thought that was all I was going to have to do.

"But that's the way it is with a broad. You get tangled up with them and they're always on your neck. So I had to take this girl's automobile and wait until George came along and then ram the car. I hated to do it, but George had been high-hatting me of late and— Well, a guy has to live."

"All right," Tragg said, "what did you do?"

"I did what I was told to," Fisk said, trembling. "I was to give it a good sideswipe. I didn't know it was going out of control and— I thought I was just framing a hit-and-run. . . . Well, that's the truth and now I've got it off my chest."

"That was Virginia Baxter's car you were using?" Mason asked.

"That's right. I was told she'd be up at the Saint's Rest and given the license number of her automobile. She hadn't much more than got into her room and got settled down than I left my car and took hers. Then, as soon as I'd done the job, I came back up and parked her car and took mine.

"The parking stall her car had been in had been taken by somebody else, so I had to park the Baxter car in a new stall. I was told to be awfully careful with that car, to give

178

the Lauretta Trent car a shove with the front end of the car, but to hit it hard with the back end so the Baxter car would run all right."

"And how much did you get for that?" Mason asked.

"Promises. I was hot. I've got enemies and I've got to get where they can't take me for a one-way ride. This broad promised me twenty-five hundred, and she gave me two hundred in cash. I don't know how you found out about me, but . . . by God, if you put me on a witness stand and the newspapers publish this stuff, my life won't be worth a snap of my fingers. . . . Hell, they're gunning for me right now. . . . You said there were two torpedoes that came up the stairs?"

Mason nodded.

Fisk held out his wrists. "Take me into custody, Lieutenant," he said. "Give me all the protection you can. I stand a chance of beating a rap, but you can't beat the big boy's torpedoes."

"Who's the big boy?" Tragg asked.

Fisk, shivering with apprehension, said, "I've never ratted on him. Always the little guys and always the outsiders; but if it comes to a showdown and I have to, I have to— Get me in a cell where I'm by myself; give me protection and a chance to take it on the lam and I'll tell."

Tragg looked at Mason, said, "Well, it seems there's butter on both sides of your bread."

Chapter 23

Mason, Della Street and Paul Drake returned to the lawyer's office shortly before midnight.

The assistant janitor who operated the elevator after
hours said, "There's been a woman trying to see you, Mr.
Mason; says it's a matter of great importance. I told her that
you said you'd be back, no matter how late it was, and she
said she'd wait."

"Where is she?"

"I don't know. Walking around somewhere. She's been
back four or five times and asked if you'd returned yet. I
told her 'no,' and she said she'd be back."

"What does she look like?" Mason asked.

"Rather aristocratic-looking. Sixty-odd. Gray hair. Nice
clothes. Quiet voice—not a crook, but something is sure
worrying her."

"All right," Mason said. "I'll be up in the office. I'm going to be there long enough for Virginia Baxter to join me;
then we're calling it a day."

"And what a day!" Paul Drake said.

"Virginia Baxter!" the elevator operator said. "You mean
the girl they're trying for murder?"

"She's being released," Mason said. "Lieutenant Tragg's
delivering her here in a police car."

"Well, what do you know?" the operator said, appraising
Mason wonderingly. "You got her out, eh?"

"*We* got her out," Mason said, grinning. "Let's go."

The elevator shot up to Mason's floor.

Drake said, "Okay, I'll duck into my office and button

things up, Perry. What are you going to do about that nurse?"

Mason grinned. "Our friend Lieutenant Tragg is taking the initiative there. You'll be reading in the papers about Tragg's brilliant deductive reasoning; probably that Tragg gave Perry Mason an opportunity to accompany him when he uncovered the key witness in the Trent murder case."

"Yes, I suppose he'll grab all the credit," Drake said.

"Tragg won't, but the department will. That's the way the game has to be played. See you in the morning, Paul."

Mason took Della Street's arm and led her down to the office.

He fitted his key to the door of his private office, switched on the lights, yawned prodigiously and walked over to the electric coffee percolator.

"How long will it be?" Della Street asked.

"Shouldn't be over ten or fifteen minutes," Mason said. "Tragg will have her out of there and leave it to me to keep her out of circulation. Tragg doesn't want anything interfering with his big story that'll hit the papers. He—"

A timid knock sounded on the corridor door.

Mason went to the door and opened it.

A tall white-haired woman said, "This is Mr. Mason?"

"Yes," Mason said.

"I couldn't wait any longer," she said. "I *had* to come to you."

She turned toward Della Street inquiringly.

"My secretary, Della Street," Mason explained, and then added, with only a moment's perceptible hesitancy, "and unless I'm very much mistaken, Della, this is Lauretta Trent."

"Exactly," she said. "I couldn't let things go to a point where that poor girl was convicted. I had to come to you.

"I'm hoping there's some way you can protect me until we can find out who is trying to murder me."

"Sit down," Mason said.

She said, "I am very naïve, Mr. Mason; I wasn't at all suspicious until Dr. Alton asked the nurse to get samples of my hair and fingernails.

"At one time I had done some research work in poisoning symptoms. I decided to get out of there and get out fast.

"Then when that car deliberately rammed us off the road and George Eagan yelled, 'Jump'—well, I jumped. I got skinned up a bit but, fortunately, I had seen that car was going to hit us and I was all ready with my hand on the door latch.

"I didn't have fifty thousand dollars in my handbag, the way you said in court, but I had enough cash so I could take care of myself.

"I saw that George was hurt. I went to the highway and, almost immediately, a motorist stopped. He took me down the road to the café. I called the highway patrol and reported the accident. They promised to have a car there right away.

"I just decided it was a good time to lie low and let things start to unscramble. I wanted to find out who was back of all this."

"And you found out?" Mason asked.

"When that will was read in court—I was never so shocked in my life."

"That will, I take it, was spurious."

"Absolutely!" she snapped. "One, or perhaps two, pages of it were genuine, the rest had been substituted. What I said in my will was that, since I had come to the conclusion that all of my relatives were barnacles simply waiting for me to die and without gumption enough to get out and do anything for themselves, I was going to give my two sisters a bequest that would be small enough so the men would have to go to work.

"I had that will in what I thought was a safe place. They must have found it, got the staples out of the pages, substituted those forged pages and decided to get rid of me."

"Apparently," Mason said, "you're due for a shock. Your relatives weren't the ones who were trying to hurry up your death, but the nurse, who was a good typist, evidently arranged with Kelvin to plant a spurious will—probably on a percentage basis with possibilities for unlimited blackmail after that.

"And in case Virginia Baxter remembered the terms of the real will, they planned to have her in such a position her testimony would be worthless.

"I'm glad you're all right. When they failed to find your handbag in the car, I had an idea you were alive.

"You've given Virginia Baxter a bad time, but it's nothing that can't be cured.

"We're waiting for Virginia Baxter to join us now."

Lauretta Trent opened her handbag. "Fortunately," she said, "I have my checkbook with me. If I made a check for twenty-five thousand dollars to you, Mr. Mason, would that take care of your fee? And, of course, a check for fifty thousand to your client to compensate her for all she's been through."

Mason grinned at Della Street. "I think if you make out the checks, Mrs. Trent, Virginia Baxter will be here by the time you've got them signed, and she can give you her answer personally."

ERLE STANLEY GARDNER
is the king of American mystery fiction.
A criminal lawyer, he filled his mystery
masterpieces with intricate, fascinating,
ever-twisting plots. Challenging, clever, and
full of surprises, these are whodunits that
have delighted mystery aficionados
for almost sixty years.

Printed in the United States
by Baker & Taylor Publisher Services